"So, what is it?"

Carrie wiped her mouth with a napkin. She looked at Massimo, only about a foot separating them on the couch. He was too close. She stood up and walked over to stand behind an armchair.

Massimo stood too. "Carrie?"

"It's nothing serious." She thought about that, then said, "Well...that's not exactly true."

Massimo frowned. "Carrie, what the—"

"I'm pregnant."

Her words hung between them. Massimo looked confused. "What did you say?"

Carrie's hands gripped the back of the seat. "I'm pregnant."

Irish author **Abby Green** ended a very glamorous career in film and TV—which really consisted of a lot of standing in the rain outside actors' trailers—to pursue her love of romance. After she'd bombarded Harlequin with manuscripts, they kindly accepted one, and an author was born. She lives in Dublin, Ireland, and loves any excuse for distraction. Visit abby-green.com or email abbygreenauthor@gmail.com.

Books by Abby Green

Harlequin Presents

Bound by Her Shocking Secret
A Ring for the Spaniard's Revenge

Passionately Ever After...

The Kiss She Claimed from the Greek

Hot Summer Nights with a Billionaire

The Flaw in His Red-Hot Revenge

The Marchetti Dynasty

The Maid's Best Kept Secret
The Innocent Behind the Scandal
Bride Behind the Desert Veil

Jet-Set Billionaires

Their One-Night Rio Reunion

Visit the Author Profile page
at Harlequin.com for more titles.

Abby Green

HIS HOUSEKEEPER'S TWIN BABY CONFESSION

HARLEQUIN

PRESENTS

HARLEQUIN®
PRESENTS™

Recycling programs
for this product may
not exist in your area.

ISBN-13: 978-1-335-59271-2

His Housekeeper's Twin Baby Confession

Copyright © 2023 by Abby Green

For questions and comments about the quality of this book,
please contact us at CustomerService@Harlequin.com.

Harlequin Enterprises ULC
22 Adelaide St. West, 41st Floor
Toronto, Ontario M5H 4E3, Canada
www.Harlequin.com

Printed in U.S.A.

HIS HOUSEKEEPER'S
TWIN BABY CONFESSION

PROLOGUE

CARRIE TAYLOR WAS too numb to be nervous about her job interview for a very prestigious job as a live-in housekeeper in London. She wasn't even sure how she'd been deemed a suitable candidate, considering her hospitality experience didn't stretch beyond working in three-star hotels in Manchester.

Clearly, going by the fact that she was in a detached Georgian mansion in one of London's most exclusive neighbourhoods, this was very much on another level. But her desire to move to London and the fact that she could start straight away because she had no ties might have had something to do with it.

No ties.

Emotion threatened to break through the numb barrier she'd pulled around herself in the last six months. She forced it down again. Not here…not now.

She would have time to lick her wounds and heal if she could just settle somewhere far away from where she'd been. At least physically, if not emotionally.

She diverted her mind from her recent traumatic past and tried to focus again on the interview. There was no way she was going to get the job. And that assertion was somehow a little liberating. A stream of considerably more glamorous and undoubtedly more experienced women had gone in before her. And one man in a three-piece suit.

They weren't wearing cheap high street clothes. Carrie plucked at her shirt, trying to straighten it. Her jacket and skirt didn't even match, but they were the same colour so that would have to do. There was a hole in her nylons, but she was hoping it wasn't visible. She'd lost almost a stone in weight in the last six months, and she really should have bought a new outfit, but she'd literally had no time to waste before coming to this interview.

The recruiter had said, 'I won't lie, it's a long shot, but nothing ventured nothing gained, eh?' And then he'd asked curiously, 'Are you sure you've never heard of Massimo Black, Lord Linden? He's the Earl of Linden.'

Carrie had shook her head, already mentally adding up how much the train ticket to London would cost. 'No, should I have?'

The recruiter had just said, 'No reason in particular, I guess…' But he'd looked at her as if she had two heads.

Carrie wondered about that now. The man was undoubtedly wealthy. And an earl, *and* a lord. Maybe he was in politics? She couldn't take her phone out here and look him up. She cursed herself for not doing it on the train when she'd had a chance. Wasn't that what people did ahead of big fancy job interviews? They swotted up on the employer?

She imagined him to be elderly and very posh. White

hair? Booming voice? The other people up for the job had certainly walked out of his office looking a little shell-shocked. Maybe he was very formidable.

'Miss Taylor?'

Carrie stood up so fast her bag fell to the floor. Flustered, she answered, 'That's me,' as she bent down to pick it up.

The stern-looking assistant swept her up and down with an icy gaze and Carrie fought not to let it affect her.

'Lord Linden will see you now. This way, please.'

She followed the young man back through the jaw-dropping reception hall, with its classic black and white tiles and a marbled staircase leading up to the first floor. There was a huge round table, polished to a high gleam. In the middle was the biggest vase she'd ever seen, with a stunning display of exotic blooms.

She was so distracted by the grandeur that she nearly ran into the man's back when he stopped abruptly outside a door. She stepped backwards. She wanted to check her hair to make sure it was still pulled neatly into its bun, but she didn't dare under his exacting gaze.

The assistant knocked and a deep voice answered, 'Come in.'

For some reason a little tingle went down Carrie's spine. The door opened and the man stood back to let her by. Carrie walked in, and for a second the sun was in her eyes, so all she could make out was a very tall, broad shape by the window.

Then she took another step and she could see. She heard herself suck in a breath. The first thing that came into her head was: *Young, not old.* And the second thing was that she'd never seen anyone more beautiful in her life. He was like a Greek statue brought to life.

Thick dark blond hair, swept back from his face. Strong jaw. Firm mouth. Powerful physique. Every line of his face and body screamed power and privilege and something far more disturbing. An earthy sensuality— an innate sexiness that she'd never experienced before.

He was saying something, but Carrie couldn't actually hear it for a moment. She tried to pull herself together. But she was shaken. This was the first time anyone or anything had pierced through the numbness in her body. And heart.

'I'm sorry, what did you say?'

Massimo Black, Lord Linden, curbed his irritation. 'I said, please take a seat.'

The woman who had just entered was looking at him as if she'd never seen a man before. He was used to slightly less obvious reactions. Maybe his assistant had been wrong when he'd said, before he went to summon her, 'This is the last one, boss, and apparently she's never heard of you.'

That had made Massimo sit up. It was rare for him to meet anyone who didn't know him and his lurid life story: inheriting the vast Linden wealth and his father's title of Earl of Linden at only eighteen, after the premature scandalous deaths of his parents—his mother of a drugs overdose at their family country pile after a debauched party and his father only a few weeks later, while piloting a helicopter with his latest lover. And then the tragic death of his beloved younger brother, who had inherited the destructive gene from his parents, in spite of Massimo's best efforts to keep him on a straight path.

Massimo pushed all that aside.

So far none of the candidates for housekeeper had impressed him, in spite of their more than adequate CVs and references. So he didn't hold out much hope for this one, who came with none of that.

The woman—he checked her name… *Carrie Taylor*—sat down gingerly on the edge of a chair. Massimo wondered why she was sitting like that, and looked down and saw she was tugging at her skirt, as if to pull it over her knee. He saw a flash of pale skin. A hole in her tights.

Massimo felt something stir in his blood. *Awareness.* He immediately scoffed at himself. For this scrap of a thing? Because she *was* a scrap. Her clothes hung off her, and she looked as if she needed to be sent to the sun for a few months, to put some colour in her cheeks.

Her blonde hair was pulled back in a bun, but tendrils were trying to escape. Her face at first glance was plain enough, but as Massimo took a seat opposite her and watched her looking around the room he could see fine bone structure, a straight nose, and a surprisingly lush mouth. Her eyes were huge, and very green. *Unusual.*

She looked at him then, and Massimo had to use all of his control to stop himself reacting.

He looked down at her file. 'It says here that you're widowed?' He looked back up just in time to see her flinch slightly.

'Yes.'

His conscience pricked. He knew what it was to lose someone you loved. The pain of his brother's death nearly ten years ago was still vivid.

'I'm sorry. It was recent?'

She avoided his eye. 'Six months ago.'

'It also says here that you're available to start right away and are available to live in?'

'Yes.'

Massimo felt curious now, about this woman who had travelled all the way from Manchester to apply for a job that she really had very little hope of getting.

He asked, 'What makes you think you'd be qualified to take on a job as housekeeper of this house?'

He saw her draw in a breath and her breasts rose under her shirt, fuller than he would have expected. He diverted his gaze up, once again incensed to be caught like this.

Affected like this.

She looked at him now, her gaze direct. Her voice was soft but clear, with a surprising hint of steel. 'I know I don't have any fancy university qualifications, but I've been working since I was sixteen.'

'Is that when you left school?'

She lifted her chin. 'Yes.'

Massimo couldn't help but admire her defiance.

She said, 'I started working in a local hotel, making beds and cleaning bathrooms, and I made it all the way up to become manager by the age of twenty. I hired staff, managed them, and was responsible for ensuring the smooth running of …everything really.'

Massimo put down her file and sat back. He found

that he could well believe it. The unmistakable pride in her voice impressed him. She didn't have an academic qualification to her name, but she had more experience in her little finger than any of the other candidates he'd just met. Who had all been as dull and boring as he might have expected.

He said, 'So my question now is, why leave all that to come and manage one house in London?'

She avoided his eye again. A shadow passed over her face. 'Because I have no ties and I would like a change. I want to gain experience in the private sector.'

Massimo had a sense that there was more to it than that, but he resisted pushing. Then he made a split-second decision—very unlike him.

He said, 'You're hired. One month's trial. My outgoing housekeeper will be on hand for a week, to show you the ropes and get you acquainted with how we run things here. How long do you need to pack up and move down?'

She looked at him, her eyes wide, dazed.

'You mean it?'

He nodded. He was fascinated by the colour coming into her cheeks. Pink. His blood grew warm. He doused it with ice. This woman would be his housekeeper. Out of bounds. If she accepted the job, from this moment on he would not allow her to affect him again.

'Um… I just need a day or two… I could be back here after the weekend?'

Massimo stood up and held out his hand. 'Perfect, my assistant will give you any help you need with packing and moving.'

* * *

Carrie couldn't quite believe what had just happened. She stood up and her legs felt shaky. She put out her hand to Lord Linden and he took it, engulfing her in heat. His touch was like an electric shock, zapping through her body and blood.

She told herself it was the shock of the job offer. And because he was so charismatic and impressive. *And young*. She'd have to be made of stone not to be affected by a man like this.

She pulled her hand back and somehow managed to get out, 'Thank you for giving me this opportunity. I'll make sure you don't regret it.'

A wave of relief went through her to think that she could move away from all the grim reminders of her life up to now. She could make a new start. In a new place. Heal herself. And maybe some day move on with her life again.

Lord Linden's gaze was hard to look away from. It was very dark. Hard to read.

Good, she told herself. She did not want to be reading this man's emotions. He was her boss, and there was too much at stake to be allowing him to affect her in any way. Emotionally or physically.

'Thank you,' she said again, and vowed to make sure that he would have no reason to regret giving her this chance.

CHAPTER ONE

Four years later

MASSIMO FELT SLIGHTLY GUILTY—but only slightly. He'd just walked out of an interview with a leading financial newspaper. The car phone rang. He looked at the display and scowled. It was one of his assistants, no doubt wondering what was going on.

He ignored it and hit the accelerator to move around some traffic, the powerful throttle of the engine doing little to lighten his mood. For that he'd need the open road and no limits on speed.

He smiled grimly. Maybe his destructive family gene was finally kicking in? The one that had taken the life of his baby brother. He'd died on a race track, chasing an impossible speed.

The journalist had irritated him from the off, asking him coquettishly how he felt about being named the richest man in the world—*again*. And then, 'Do you feel a responsibility to ensure that the next generation carries on your legacy of philanthropy?'

In other words, would he be settling down and having

children? He was hardly going to confide in a journalist that he had no intention of siring another generation of Lindens. Not after the sterling example his parents had provided with their destructive, chaotic parenting.

He and his brother had been farmed out to nannies and boarding schools. There had been little to no consistency in their lives. The effect on Massimo, as the eldest, had been to make him develop a strong sense of responsibility. A desire to have structure and create order from chaos.

His younger brother had gone the other way, taking after their parents. Massimo had often wondered if he'd been less careful, would his brother have felt the need to rebel? But that way lay madness.

In any case, Massimo had the reckless blood of his Italian countess mother and his feckless playboy father in his veins too, and no way was he going to risk passing it down to another generation. He'd watched his brother crash and burn—literally. He wouldn't do that to his own child.

He chose his lovers scrupulously and only spent one night with them, so there could never be a hint of anything more. After witnessing his father decimate what little self-confidence his mother had had, by taking lovers without even trying to hide it, Massimo had no desire to test his own ability to be faithful. He wouldn't risk doing that to a woman.

So far, one night had always been enough. Well, up until about six months ago. Since then… He hadn't had the appetite.

Massimo drove through the electronic gates of his

London home. The prickliness of his exchange with the journalist faded as he stepped out of the car. The late summer city air was still. He walked to his front door and it opened as if operated by some kind of magical device.

But there was no magical device—just his housekeeper, Miss Taylor, on the threshold. She was dressed in her usual uniform of black short-sleeved shirt and black trousers. Flat shoes. Blonde hair pulled back neatly in a bun at the base of her neck. No overt make-up. No jewellery.

And there it was. That little beat in his blood. *Awareness*. No matter how much he tried to ignore it or push it down. And lately it had been harder to ignore.

She held the door open. 'Welcome back, sir.' She frowned a little. 'I wasn't expecting you back this early…is everything all right?'

The irritation prickled back to life. Was his life so regimented, so predictable, that he couldn't even come back to his own home ahead of time? And that was strange, because Miss Taylor was one of the few people who didn't irritate him.

No, she had a unique effect on him. It was a mix of that illicit awareness and something far more disturbing…like a balm. How could he be both aware of someone and feel calmed by them? It was ridiculous. He was losing it.

She'd worked for him for four years now, and he'd often congratulated himself on trusting his gut and hiring her. She'd become one of his most trusted employees. And, as such, he was about to request of her that she do him a massive favour.

He said, 'Actually, there's something I need to ask you. Can you come to my office?'

Carrie didn't know why she hesitated for a second, but when Lord Linden looked at her pointedly she said, 'Of course.'

She dutifully followed him to his study and tried not to notice the way he effortlessly filled out his three-piece suit. His hair was curling a little over his collar, and Carrie had the most bizarre urge to touch it and comment that it was getting long.

She could sense he was in a strange mood because she could always sense his moods—like some kind of unwelcome sixth sense. And, really, the man wasn't at all moody. He could be brooding, yes. But he never took it out on staff.

He went into his study and she followed, closing the door behind her. This was where she'd had her interview. Strange to think that had been four years ago. A surge of emotion surprised her. This job had provided her with everything she'd hoped for. A place to settle and start healing a little.

Her inconvenient awareness of her boss had been manageable up till now. She generally avoided eye contact if at all possible, and their conversations were always centred around the house and schedules. And he travelled for work. A lot. Sometimes he could be away for up to a month at a time.

But in the last few months he hadn't been travelling

so much. He'd been in London more. And seeing him
almost every day had begun to wear on Carrie's nerves
a little. Her sense of control around him was starting to
fray, as if mocking her for thinking she had anything
under control.

'Please, sit down, Miss Taylor.'

Carrie sat down, not sure what Lord Linden wanted
to talk to her about. He sat down behind his desk, somehow still dominating the space even though he was no
longer standing.

He hadn't taken a lover in months.

That random and incendiary thought popped into
Carrie's head. She blushed. What was going on with
her today? What did she care if he'd taken a lover lately
or not?

*Because it bothers you to see them the morning after
and send them on their way.*

Carrie fought to regain her composure. Maybe he'd
been taking his lovers to a hotel? Or sleeping over in
their apartments?

'Is everything all right?' Lord Linden asked.

Carrie nodded and said, 'Fine…just fine. It's a bit
warm, that's all.'

Lord Linden got up again and opened the window
that looked out over a lush back garden. A total luxury in central London. Carrie wasn't looking at that,
though. She was mesmerised by the play of muscles
under his suit.

He looked at her. 'Better?'

She was definitely losing it. 'Yes, thank you.'

He sat down again. Carrie clasped her hands together, praying she wouldn't betray herself again.

He said, 'You know I'm due to go to New York tomorrow?'

She'd actually forgotten. A wave of relief went through her. 'Yes—for a week, isn't it?'

'Possibly longer, actually. But there's an issue. My regular housekeeper who looks after the Manhattan apartment has retired early, due to ill health. So far my team haven't found anyone suitable. I have to entertain while I'm there—a small drinks party—and I'd like to feel that things are being taken care of...properly.'

Carrie's relief drained away. She wasn't sure where this was going.

Lord Linden sat forward. 'I was hoping that you might consider coming with me.'

The relief drained away and Carrie felt panicky. 'Go to New York? With you?'

He nodded. 'To work in my apartment as housekeeper for the duration of my trip. Hopefully by the time I leave we'll have found a replacement.'

Carrie clasped her hands even tighter. 'I... I don't really know what to say. I've never been to America. I wouldn't know the first thing about how things work over there.'

She was beset by a million things. Disbelief, confusion, terror and, probably most disturbingly, excitement. This was exactly what she *didn't* need. More time in Lord Linden's company!

He looked at her, supremely at ease. 'Is your passport up to date?'

She nodded. 'I just had it renewed recently.'

An old habit that she hadn't let go of.

'That's all you need.'

He made it sound so simple. Not a big deal. He was just transplanting her from here to there.

But then you'll have no peace.

She would be in even closer proximity to him at a time when she felt as if she was losing her sense of control around him. It would be madness to go...and yet she didn't really have a choice.

Nevertheless, she resisted. 'But won't you need me here?'

Lord Linden responded easily. 'You've ensured this property runs like clockwork. I think it can do without you for a week or two. As I said, I have an important event to host at my apartment. I would appreciate having someone I trust there to oversee things. You don't need to worry about the minutiae—my assistant in New York will work to your orders.'

She absorbed this. And then, 'A week or two?'

He nodded. 'Until my commitments there are finished. I'm sure that by then my team will have sourced a new housekeeper.'

She said it out loud. 'I guess I don't really have a choice?'

He arched a brow. 'Would it really be so terrible to spend a couple of weeks in New York? You'll have time off to do whatever you wish.'

Carrie knew that if she said no it would be weird. She was his London housekeeper. What he was asking of her was perfectly reasonable. And it was New York. She'd never travelled much beyond the UK at all.

'Okay, yes. I'll go with you.'

Lord Linden said crisply, 'Good. We'll be leaving before lunch tomorrow. I trust that'll be enough time to get your things together and ensure the house is left in good hands?'

'Of course,' Carrie answered smoothly.

Maybe this was all in her head and she was just being ridiculous.

'Very good. That'll be all, Miss Taylor.'

Carrie hurried out before she made a total fool of herself.

Four years working for this man without a ripple and suddenly it felt as if a storm was brewing.

Carrie had only ever been on a plane a couple of times before, and never on a private jet. She thought she'd become accustomed to luxurious living in Lord Linden's London house, but the sleek jet mocked her for being so complacent.

The interior was cream and gold. Plush soft carpets. The chair she sat in felt as if it had been contoured especially to fit her body. It was beyond decadent.

She sat towards the front of the jet and Lord Linden sat behind her at a desk with his laptop, working. Throughout the flight she'd been offered any beverage she would like, and a menu featuring the kind of food usually served at one of Lord Linden's dinner parties. She'd settled for sparkling water.

She was too keyed up to sleep, so she alternated

between looking at the clouds out of the window and flicking through a magazine she wasn't reading. After a couple of hours she noticed that she hadn't heard the low rumble of Lord Linden's voice in a while.

Feeling like a voyeur, she sneaked a look behind her and saw that he was sitting—no, sprawling—with long legs stretched out across the aisle under his table, reading a document with a small frown between his eyes.

With his collar open and shirtsleeves rolled up, his hair messy as if he'd run a hand through it, and stubble on his jaw, he looked as if he should be swilling champagne with a beautiful woman on each arm—not reading a report. The man oozed sex appeal in a way that Carrie suspected he didn't even appreciate.

Oh, he knew he had it—that was obvious in every move he made—but there was something else…an air of jaded insouciance that gave his appeal another edge. He seemed so utterly arrogant and aloof all at once. It was an intoxicating combination, and doubtless one that drew women in droves.

Not her, though. She knew better.

As if sensing her intense focus on him, he looked up, and Carrie was too slow to escape that dark gaze. She gulped and could feel heat rising into her cheeks.

A small voice mocked her. *Sure you're so in control?*

His gaze narrowed on her. 'Everything okay?'

She nodded. 'Fine…just fine, thank you.' He put down his sheaf of papers and she said hurriedly, 'Sorry, I didn't mean to disturb you, Lord Linden.'

He looked at her steadily. 'You don't need to keep calling me Lord Linden.'

She'd been calling him that for four years.

Carrie contained her surprise. 'I... Okay.' She couldn't possibly call him by his name. It reminded her too much of the lovers she had to help dispatch the morning after...'

'Did Massimo leave me a message?'

He hasn't taken a lover in months, that sly voice reminded her.

Carrie pushed it down desperately. She asked, 'What should I call you?'

'Call me Massimo.'

Carrie blanched. 'Are you sure that's...appropriate?'

Her boss frowned at her. 'It is if I say it is. Lord Linden makes me feel old and stuffy, and I don't think I'm either of those things, do you?'

Looking at him in that elegant, sexy sprawl, Carrie couldn't help saying, 'No.'

His gaze slid to her table. 'No champagne?'

Carrie straightened. 'It's the middle of the day.'

A small smile played around the corner of his mouth. 'Well, it's actually evening now.'

She felt exposed. Gauche. Boundaries set in stone for four years seemed to be dissolving around her.

'You're not drinking,' she said.

The faint smile disappeared. 'I don't really drink all that much.'

No, he didn't. Carrie had often observed him at parties in his own home, where he would stand on the edge of the crowd holding a glass of sparkling wine, but not drinking it. There was a drinks cabinet in his study, full of some of the world's most expensive and exclusive whiskies, and it was hardly touched.

He always looked brooding at those parties. Unapproachable. But inevitably there would be a stream of women who *did* approach, not taking his air of impermeability as anything but encouragement.

Carrie was about to say, *I should let you get back to work*, but instead what came out of her mouth was, 'Would it be okay if you called me Carrie? Miss Taylor makes me feel like a schoolteacher.'

For a moment she thought she might have overstepped the mark, in spite of his request for her to use his first name. But then he said, 'That would be absolutely okay.'

'Thank you. I should let you get back to work.'

For a moment he said nothing, and then, 'You're probably right… Carrie.'

She turned around again before he could see the heat in her face. They'd exchanged more words in the past twenty-four hours than they had in the whole term of her employment. And now they were on a first-name basis. She felt giddy again.

But she needed to remember that she was just here because her boss needed her to *work* in New York.

Driving into Manhattan was sensory overload for Carrie. She couldn't get over the buildings towering over the wide streets. The chaos of the traffic, horns honking constantly. The sheer number of people.

She felt eyes on her and looked to her right, where Massimo sat on the other side of the SUV.

He was looking at her. 'Okay?' he said.

Carrie felt like shaking her head. Her heart-rate was about triple its usual speed. They'd just taken a helicopter from the airport to a rooftop in Manhattan, and had then been met by this chauffeur-driven car down at street level. She couldn't pretend she was au fait with what was happening.

She smiled ruefully. 'I wasn't expecting a helicopter ride into the most famous city in the world.'

Massimo shrugged. 'It's expedient when I have a lot to do in a short space of time.'

'Of course,' Carrie murmured.

She'd almost forgotten who she was dealing with here. It wasn't as if it was for her benefit.

'The driver is going to drop me at my offices and take you on to the apartment, if that's all right? The concierge has been instructed to let you in and show you around, and my assistant will come over later to give you a full briefing on the event I'm hosting and what's required.'

Butterflies erupted in Carrie's gut. She was used to dealing with high society in London, but Manhattan was a whole other level.

'Okay.' Impulsively she added, 'Look, I don't want to let you down—are you sure you want me to take care of this?'

'I trust you and your judgement. You'll be fine.'

He meant in a professional capacity, of course. Not personally. But Carrie couldn't stop the little glow in her chest. She knew how exacting her boss was.

The car was slowing now, and it came to a stop outside a vertiginous steel building. Even when Carrie craned her neck at the window she couldn't see all the way to the top.

Before he got out Massimo said, 'I'll be working late, so feel free to do whatever you like. We can discuss things tomorrow morning.'

Carrie felt like pointing out that he didn't have to tell her his movements, but instead she just nodded.

Massimo uncoiled his large body from the back of the car and immediately left a vacuum behind. Carrie watched him stride into the building in his three-piece suit, not one inch of him looking as if he'd just got off a transatlantic flight.

Carrie grimaced. When she'd dressed much earlier that morning in a dark trouser suit and short-sleeved light woollen top, flat brogues, hair coiled up into a chignon, she'd hoped to project a coolly professional image. Now she felt thoroughly wrinkled and badly in need of refreshing.

Even though it was late summer, almost tipping into autumn season, she hadn't expected the heat in Manhattan to be so intense. She'd only been outside in between transferring into different vehicles, but in spite of the air-conditioned car she could still feel perspiration on her lower back and the back of her neck.

Not long after dropping Massimo at his office the car turned down a wide street that was immediately less frenetic. When they emerged at the other end Carrie could see a leafy green park ahead of them.

She leant forward to ask the driver, 'Is that Central Park?'

'Yes, ma'am.'

The car turned onto a street bordering the park and came to a stop outside another impossibly tall building—except where Massimo's office had been all sleek modernity, this building oozed old Manhattan grandeur. When she got out of the vehicle and looked across the road she noticed the iconic address: Fifth Avenue.

Of course.

A man in uniform hurried out from under the awning of the building and said, 'Miss Taylor?'

She nodded and smiled, feeling the heat quickly enveloping her.

'I'm Matt, the concierge. I've been instructed to show you around Mr Black's apartment.'

Carrie allowed him to lead her into a blessedly cool marbled reception area. There was a massive round table holding a vase of opulent blooms the size of a small tree. The air was subtly perfumed.

Matt led her into an elevator and as the doors closed said conspiratorially, 'This is Mr Black's private elevator. He owns the whole building, but he just uses the top floor for himself.'

'You don't have to call him Lord Linden, then?' Carrie observed.

The older man shrugged. 'He prefers not.'

Carrie absorbed that nugget. Maybe he appreciated the relative anonymity and more relaxed social protocols of America. The elevator doors opened into a reception hall that oozed classic sophistication. Tiled floors and panelled walls. Doors leading off in different directions.

The concierge led her over to one and opened it. It was only because Carrie was used to Massimo's London house that she didn't gasp out loud. She'd never seen ceilings so high nor windows so huge. She walked over to a window to see the green expanse of Central Park laid out before her. And there was a terrace beyond the windows, lined with flowering plants.

The furnishings were opulent, but understated. This was obviously a formal reception room, with different seating areas, chairs and couches around low coffee tables, upon which sat various massive hardback tomes featuring art, photography and architecture.

There were numerous antiques and a lot of art was hung on the walls. Carrie wouldn't have been able to name the artist, but she recognised one painting of a Parisian scene featuring a woman that must undoubtedly be an original.

'If you come this way I'll show you where the kitchen and utility rooms are, and also your private rooms.'

Carrie flushed. For a second there she had almost been imagining herself inhabiting this space as a visitor, not an employee.

She followed Matt out of the room and down another plush corridor. He led her up some stairs and opened a door into a kitchen that made Carrie gasp audibly. It was stunning—state of the art. A gleaming marble-topped central island was surrounded by acres of countertops. There was a Belfast sink. A cooker that looked as if it could launch a satellite. And a walk-in pantry, stocked to the gills—as was the massive fridge.

'I was told to let you know that the chef will work to your instructions when you have them.'

Mute with awe, Carrie reluctantly left the kitchen and followed Matt again. He deftly showed her an informal media room that looked more like a home cinema. A formal dining room. A gym with a lap pool. And then an elevator door which Matt pointed to and said, 'That brings you up to Mr Black's sleeping quarters, his office and the rooftop terrace.'

There was also an entertaining space the size of a small ballroom with French doors leading out onto a wide terrace and a wrought-iron staircase that led to the rooftop terrace on the upper level.

It was dizzying…the sheer scale of the apartment over three floors.

'And these are your rooms, Miss Taylor.'

The man opened a door with a flourish and Carrie walked inside, taking in a huge bedroom, en suite bathroom and walk-in closet. French doors led out to a balcony, with jaw-dropping views over the park.

'Please help yourself to anything in the kitchen. The phone in the reception hall will dial directly down to me if you need anything. I believe your luggage will be arriving soon.'

Carrie turned around, feeling overwhelmed and seriously doubtful that she'd ever find her way back to that reception hall. 'Thank you, Matt.'

The man ducked his head and was gone, leaving her alone in the vast space. She went over to the French doors and opened them, stepping out onto her own private balcony with sweeping views across Central Park.

Carrie shook her head and smiled wryly.

Not bad for a housekeeper.

Not bad for a girl who had grown up on a council estate with a single mother who had worked her fingers to the bone to provide for them both.

Carrie's mother had never hidden the truth of her birth, once she was old enough to understand. Her father had seduced her mother into an affair, but as soon as she'd fallen pregnant he'd revealed he was married and had dumped her. Carrie had never met him, but she knew he'd had a family of his own the whole time he'd been with her mother.

The stain of abandonment was something she could never fully wash away, no matter how much her mother had tried to make up for it, and it had left a weak spot in her self-esteem. A weak spot that had been exploited and manipulated when she'd been at her most vulnerable, after her mother had died.

That was when her husband had come along and made her believe he could heal the hurt places inside her...give her a life that she'd only imagined in her most private moments. A family. Unconditional love. Security.

But it had all been a toxic lie.

Carrie forced unwelcome thoughts of the past out of her head and rested her arms on the stone wall, taking in the view...the verdant green and the tall, elegant buildings on the other side of the park that mirrored the one she was in. The sounds from the street far below barely even permeated the rarefied air up here.

She wandered back through the apartment and stood at the doors of the elevator that went to the upper floor. Telling herself she was only doing her job by acquainting herself with everything, Carrie got inside, and the lift ascended silently, its doors opening again with a melodic *ping*.

She entered a corridor much like the one she'd just left, except up here there was only a couple of doors, one at the end. She walked to it and hesitated, before telling herself she was being ridiculous. She routinely had to go into her boss's bedroom in London, for various reasons.

She opened the door. His scent immediately hit her nostrils. Dark and woodsy and something like…leather. The room was vast and dressed in dark earthen tones. A massive bed dominated the space, but she avoided looking at that and investigated further to find an en suite bathroom and a walk-in closet.

There was also a lounge area, with a TV and floor-to-ceiling bookshelves. They contained mostly non-fiction books on economics and business, and some thrillers and light fiction. Carrie couldn't imagine Massimo sitting still for long enough to relax and read. The man had an electric energy about him.

She was turning to leave when she saw some photos on a table, framed. She walked over and picked one up. It showed a young man—gorgeous, but not Massimo— with a wide smile, dressed in a motor racing suit standing beside a car, holding up a trophy. Carrie knew that her boss had had a younger brother who'd died tragically on the racing track.

She put the picture back, feeling even more like a voyeur. She'd looked her boss up after she'd been offered the job, and knew about as much as any of the general public did about his infamously tragic family history. His brother's death had been only the tip of the iceberg...

His mother had been a stunningly beautiful Italian countess and his father the aristocratic heir to one of Europe's biggest estates. The Earl and Countess of Linden had lived a fast and glamorous life, rarely out of the papers with their tempestuous relationship, allegations of affairs, and more sordid rumours of drugs and gambling.

Massimo's mother had died of a suspected drug overdose on the family estate outside London, and then a year later his father had died in a helicopter crash en route to a casino in Monte Carlo. The fact that he'd been flying the helicopter, and had been responsible for the death of his young and beautiful lover—another European aristocrat—had only added to the reams of newsprint about the ill-fated family.

As far as Carrie had been able to make out Massimo would have only been eighteen and his younger brother sixteen at the time his father had died.

The current Earl of Linden certainly hadn't inherited his family's excesses. Quite the opposite. His lifestyle was positively monk-like in comparison.

Monk-like, and yet he didn't make Carrie think of chaste monks…

She felt warm all of a sudden, and spied more French doors leading out onto what had to be the rooftop terrace. She opened them and went outside to a vast, breathtaking space that gave even more spectacular views than the level below.

'Not bad, hmm?'

Carrie whirled around. Massimo was standing behind her, tie off, shirt open at his throat, hands in his pockets. She felt caught. Exposed. Hot.

'I'm sorry, I shouldn't be up here. I was just…exploring,' she finished lamely.

Being nosy, more like, said a little tart voice.

He walked towards where she stood by the wall. 'I've asked you here as my housekeeper—this is your domain.'

She turned around to face the view and gulped. The apartment might be her domain, but his private suite was *not* her domain and never would be.

'You need to know the layout.'

Carrie appreciated his diplomacy. 'Your concierge told me this floor was your private suite.'

'But it's also the roof terrace, where I will be hosting my function tomorrow night.'

She looked at him, her heart palpitating. 'Tomorrow night?'

He nodded. 'I've come back early to work from my office here—it's less distracting. One of my assistants is with me…he's in the lounge downstairs. He'll go through the week's events with you and give you all the information you need for the smooth running of the apartment.'

'I'll go straight down and meet him.'

She turned and left, eager for an excuse to get out of Massimo's orbit, and cursing herself for allowing her curiosity to get the better of her.

CHAPTER TWO

THE FOLLOWING EVENING Carrie's equilibrium was slightly restored. She was back in her comfort zone—directing operations for the drinks party Massimo was hosting.

His assistant had described it as a fairly low-key event, consisting of drinks and canapés, but the organisation involved to make it all look as effortless as possible resembled a minor military operation.

Carrie had seen the guest list and it was most definitely *not* low-key. Some of the names had made her gasp out loud. An ex-United States President... One of the world's best-loved actresses... She'd seen plenty of A-listers in her time at events in the house in London, but this was another level of intimidating.

Thankfully an events team were taking care of everything, so all she had to do was supervise and liaise between the events company and Massimo's own staff.

The party was taking place between the ballroom and the roof terrace, with guests moving back and forth. Now Carrie was making her way up to the terrace, moving unobtrusively through the crowd. She was wearing her habitual events uniform: a black sleeveless shift dress and black court shoes, a string of faux pearls around her neck. Her hair was up and pulled back into a low bun.

The dress code for the guests was cocktail wear and, surrounded by women in a glittering array of colourful slinky dresses, Carrie faded into the background exactly as she preferred to do. Or as she *had* always preferred to do.

For the first time in her life at an event like this, she was ashamed to admit that she felt slightly envious of the women in their sparkling dresses. Yet the thought of being front and centre in a crowd like this, with everyone looking at her, made her go clammy with horror.

She hovered on the edge of the crowd, her expert eye taking everything in and noting that all was running smoothly. She tried desperately not to let her gaze go to where Massimo stood, head and shoulders above almost everyone around him, but it was next to impossible.

He was magnificent in a dark suit, a lighter coloured silk tie and white shirt. The dim lights made his hair look darker. His arms were folded as he listened intently to what someone was saying to him and his muscles bunched under the expensive material. As if his suit couldn't contain him…

An electric pulse zinged through her blood. There was something so illicitly thrilling about how sexual he was underneath the civilised veneer.

Carrie went hot and then cold as that disturbing thought registered. She'd never considered herself a sexual person—her husband had certainly tried and failed to arouse her…she'd always found sex painful and somehow demeaning…and yet here she was, ogling her boss like a hormonal teenager.

Carrie impulsively took a tray full of canapés from one of the wait staff to help out with serving. She needed a reminder of why she was here.

'So, you see, without the funds you provided we absolutely wouldn't be where we are today, and it's thanks to the Linden Foundation that…'

Massimo tuned out the voice again.

Where was she?

Even though he was surrounded by some of the most charismatic, powerful, interesting and beautiful people in the world, he wasn't interested in them.

He looked over the heads of the guests around him and a flash of blonde hair caught his peripheral vision. He turned to look and his blood leapt in reaction. A reaction that no other woman here had elicited.

She had her back to him and was wearing the plainest dress imaginable. Perfectly appropriate, of course, but it irritated Massimo. She was offering canapés to his guests and handing them napkins.

Without thinking about what he was doing, he murmured something into the constant flow of his companion's words and moved away, instantly feeling a sense of relief. *And anticipation.*

He walked up behind Carrie and took her arm lightly in his hand. He could feel her muscles. She was strong. She looked at him, and he saw the way she flushed.

Awareness. Not just him.

Satisfaction rolled through him in a way he hadn't experienced in a long time.

He took the tray with his free hand and handed it to a passing waiter. Then he led Carrie to a quiet spot. She turned to face him. Reluctantly he let her arm go.

'What are you doing?' he asked.

He noticed that her mouth was very soft. Pink. No lipstick. It was a beautiful shape. Naturally pouting. Her eyes were huge and very green. He felt as if he'd been underestimating just how beautiful she was for a long time, and now he was being punished for it.

'I'm just helping out.'

'There are staff here for that.'

'I don't mind.'

I do.

Massimo just about stopped himself from saying those words. He had a very strong sense that he never wanted to see her in a role of subservience again.

This was unprecedented. He *never* got involved with staff. He trusted them to do their jobs—none more so than this woman. If she'd decided to lend a hand then he was sure she'd had good reason to. He was exposing himself.

He took a step back. Became aware of the crowd around them. Eyes on him. 'Of course. I trust your judgement.'

Carrie watched Massimo turn and walk back into the crowd, swallowed up in seconds by people clamouring for his attention. She was still trembling from the way he had put his hand on her and led her aside. Her skin burned as if from a brand.

It was crazy, but it was the closest proximity she'd had to a man in a long time. And it had brought up a multitude of emotions and sensations, none of which she had expected, considering the fact that her husband had been so abusive. Never physically, although the threat had always been there, but mentally and verbally.

For the first time in a long time excitement flowed through her veins—not fear or disgust.

For years she'd avoided physical contact with people, which was easy enough to do in a work environment and when you didn't have a partner. Usually if someone touched her she tensed, recoiled. But as soon as *he'd* touched her she'd known it was him.

She'd welcomed his touch.

The realisation made her feel light-headed. For the last four years she'd carried the fear that she would never be able to allow someone physically close again. Not to mention emotionally.

Absorbing this revelation distracted Carrie from thinking too much about why Massimo hadn't wanted to see her serving his guests in the first place. She would unpick that later.

The events manager caught her eye and came over. 'Sorry to disturb you, Miss Taylor, but the chef wants a word?'

Carrie welcomed the diversion and fled.

* * *

The rest of the evening was a blur as Carrie threw herself into activity, doing her best to avoid going back up to the terrace.

When people started to leave, the events manager found her and smiled. 'Thanks for all your help, Miss Taylor. We can take care of things from here.'

Carrie took her cue and went to her rooms. She didn't want to witness Massimo choosing a woman to spend the night with. She would find out in the morning when she checked the bedrooms, no doubt. He might not have taken a lover in London for some time now, but she was sure New York would provide him with fresh... *inspiration.*

Carrie scowled at herself in her bathroom mirror. She'd changed into her pyjamas—shorts and a short-sleeved shirt—and her hair was long and tangled around her shoulders. She looked about as far away as it was possible to get from one of Massimo's sultry lovers.

She couldn't hear a thing from the party in her rooms—the apartment was well sound-proofed. She got into bed, but felt too restless to sleep. She got up again, pulled on a short dressing gown and went out onto her balcony.

The music had stopped but she could still hear conversation and sporadic bursts of laughter. Was Massimo with a woman now? A woman he had chosen? Looking at her? Touching her? Surely he would smile when he seduced a woman?

Carrie was surprised at the jealousy that rose up inside her. She had no right to be jealous of any woman.

She took a deep breath and tried to calm her restlessness. She had to admit that in the space of the last few days she'd tipped over the edge of being acceptably aware of her boss in a way that hadn't affected her too much, into full-on crush territory.

It was as if a Pandora's box had opened inside her and four years of repressed emotions and longings were being brought back to life.

It had been a long time since she'd felt like this and it troubled her. Because the last time it had ended in a marriage that had reduced her to a shell of the person she'd been.

She'd had to work hard in the intervening years to try to forgive herself for letting her husband into her life. For trusting him and allowing him to wage upon her a slow and insidious campaign of abuse that had worn her down.

They'd met just after her mother had died, when Carrie had been at her most vulnerable and feeling very alone in the world. Her mother's death had made her even more acutely aware that her absent father had chosen his own family over her. Her mother had been her rock and her guide, and without her Carrie's strength had felt very shaky.

Her husband, a master manipulator, had sensed that and exploited it. Carrie knew this wasn't her fault, and she knew that women even stronger than her had been taken in in similar ways, but the reflex to blame herself for being weak was still strong. Strong enough to let her relish working as a housekeeper for a man whose house was like a fortress, and which had provided her with much needed space and time to heal.

And she *had* healed—on many levels. Perhaps this ridiculous growing desire for her boss should just be taken as a welcome sign that she was ready to open up a part of herself that she'd locked away for a long time.

She'd vowed never to marry again, because she knew she could never trust anyone that much, but she hadn't ruled out the possibility of a relationship. Companionship. Maybe this fascination with her boss was her body's way of telling her that she was ready for the next step in her healing. As terrifying as that thought was…

The morning after the party, Massimo answered a call in his home office with a disgruntled-sounding, 'Yes?'

It was his executive assistant, informing him that one of the guests from the party—a famous model—wanted to know if Massimo had a date for the charity ball at the end of the week, and if not could she offer herself?

Massimo would never cease to be shocked by the ways and means and audacity of women looking to get his attention. He couldn't even picture the woman in question.

'No,' he responded. 'I do not wish to accept her kind offer of a date.'

'So you'll be going solo?'

Massimo stood up and walked over to the window. He was feeling restless. He hadn't seen Carrie yet that morning. One of the other staff had served him at breakfast. He'd looked for her at the end of the party last night, but one of the events staff had informed him chirpily that she'd gone to bed.

There was no reason for that fact to have irked Massimo so much. Carrie would routinely slip away before the end of a party, once it was largely over and in the capable hands of the events manager. But it had irked him last night.

Impulsively he said, 'Actually, I already have a date.'

'You do?'

The incredulity in his assistant's tone made Massimo scowl. He couldn't help but be acutely aware that his lack of interest in taking a lover lately had become a fevered source of speculation.

Hence why the plan he was now considering would be the perfect solution. A way to curb the gossips while also proving to himself that this sudden fascination for his housekeeper was an anomaly.

'Yes, I do,' he repeated, pushing aside the pricking of his conscience.

He cut off the connection and threw the phone back onto the table behind him. He stuck his hands in his pockets. He couldn't deny that he was behaving completely out of character, and that this plan would potentially blur the boundaries between him and his housekeeper, but for the first time in his life he chose not to think about the consequences.

'Would you join me for lunch?'

Carrie's mouth fell open.

She'd just shown Massimo out onto the terrace, where she'd laid a table for lunch. A light chicken salad and crusty bread. He was looking at her, perfectly composed, as if he hadn't just asked her a preposterous thing.

'I…' She was about to tell a white lie and say that she'd already eaten when something reckless moved through her. *Temptation.* 'Okay.'

'Good.' He went and sat down.

In a bit of a daze, Carrie got another place setting and went out to the table. There was more than enough food for two. Maybe Massimo was just being practical. He had always erred on the side of discretion and frugality over ostentation. Perhaps in reaction to the lurid and lavish ways of his parents and brother.

Massimo helped himself to a portion of salad and handed her the utensils.

'Thank you.'

Carrie still felt dazed. What was she doing, sitting at a table with her boss, dressed in her very plain uniform of white shirt and black trousers, flat shoes. Hair pulled back, as always. Minimal make-up.

He hadn't taken a lover last night. Or at least there had been no evidence of breakfast for two. Carrie hated how relieved she felt. This crush was becoming ridiculous.

'You prefer working here to the office?' she asked, aiming for polite interest.

'I would be inundated with requests and interruptions there. I'll spend some time there once I've got my actual work done.'

Carrie swallowed a mouthful of food, too self-conscious to meet Massimo's eye. 'I'd never realised the amount of work there is in philanthropy. Surely it's easier to give money away than to make it?'

'You would think…'

She glanced at him now, because he sounded so grim, and saw he was looking at her.

He said, 'It turns out that giving money away involves almost as much as trying to make it, and the responsibility for who to give it to and when is more complicated and delicate than negotiating a peace agreement between two warring countries.'

Curious now, Carrie asked, 'Do you actually…*enjoy* it?'

Massimo blinked and sat back, as if surprised by her question. 'No one has ever asked me that before. I like giving the money away… I don't much like all the bureaucracy and politics that comes with it.'

'At least you can have a clear conscience.'

His gaze narrowed on her then. 'Actually, I have an ulterior motive for inviting you to dine with me. I need a favour. Another favour.'

Carrie put down her fork. For no good reason her heart-rate had doubled. 'A favour?' What on earth could she possibly do for the man who literally had everything?

He nodded. 'There's an event at the end of the week—a charity ball. I need a date and I would appreciate it if you'd consider coming with me.'

I need a date.

Arguably the wealthiest man in the world, and inarguably one of the most gorgeous, wanted *her* to accompany him as his date?

Carrie shook her head, as if that might make sense of what he'd just said. 'Why on earth would you want *me* to come with you?'

'Because, quite frankly, I don't want to bring a date who might be under the impression that anything else is on offer.'

'You mean like…?' The word *sex* hovered on her tongue but then Massimo spoke.

'Like a relationship.'

Carrie could feel a hot flush rising.

Of course.

Maybe that was why he hadn't taken a lover in months—because his lovers inevitably wanted more.

His offer—*suggestion*—was causing a maelstrom inside her. A mixture of girlish excitement, which was entirely inappropriate, and terror and exhilaration. And yet more terror. Mainly terror. And confusion.

'Wouldn't it be a little…unorthodox?'

He gave a small shrug. 'It doesn't have to be. It would obviously be considered as out-of-hours work for you. You'll be well recompensed.'

Immediately the heat inside her cooled. Of course. He just wanted her to act as a buffer. She remembered the crowd around him the previous evening, clamouring for his attention.

The stark facts that she had grown up on a council estate and left school early made her no match for the kind of people he socialised with. She had to face reality: she would be a liability. Not to mention the thought of the scrutiny she would face being on his arm. Every flaw exposed!

She shook her head. 'I'm sorry, but I really don't think I can do that.'

Massimo took a bite of his salad, seemingly unconcerned. 'Why?'

'I've never been in that kind of situation before. I wouldn't have a clue how to behave. What if someone talks to me?'

'You talk back—they're just human beings.'

Carrie made a noise. 'To you, maybe… It's different for someone like me.'

'What do you mean?'

Carrie pushed her plate away. There was no way she could eat now. 'To those people someone like me is invisible. I'm just there to top up a drink or serve food or clean up after them.'

'You mean people like me?'

Carrie flushed. 'Well…yes, but you're different…'

Massimo acknowledged all his employees in a way that she knew most others didn't.

'You don't sound bitter about it,' he responded.

Carrie looked at him. 'I'm not. I've never expected anything else. I wouldn't want your life if you paid me.'

She realised what she'd said and put a hand to her mouth, a nervous giggle escaping. She took her hand down.

'That's literally what you're proposing to do. To pay me to be in your world.'

'What's so bad about my life, then?'

Massimo sat back and Carrie wanted to kick herself. How on earth had they got *here*?

'I guess in many ways it's not bad—you have everything you could ever want… But I think, if I'm not speaking too much out of turn, it's isolating. I don't see you having much…fun.'

'Do *you* have fun?' There was no sharpness to the question, as if she'd offended him, just curiosity.

Carrie felt self-conscious. 'I don't suppose I can claim to have much fun…no.'

'So maybe we're not that different after all.'

She'd never thought about it like that.

He continued, 'And maybe it might be considered fun to dress up and come with me to something you've never experienced before?'

Before she could even acknowledge how adroitly he was manoeuvring her Carrie thought of something far scarier. She thought of the women at the party the previous night, in cocktail dresses of every hue, with gems glittering from ears, necks and hands. She thought of how she'd envied them.

'In any case, I don't have anything remotely suitable to wear.'

Massimo waved a hand. 'That's easily taken care of.'

Carrie was rendered momentarily speechless. 'But… I'm your housekeeper.'

'Like I said, you'd be doing me a favour.'

He was saying all this in such a reasonable way that Carrie felt she would be overreacting if she kept protesting. Her boss wanted her to go to an event as his date—in a work capacity—in order to keep him from the hordes of women.

For a moment Carrie wondered if she might actually

be dreaming. Or hallucinating. She wanted to pinch herself, and did so under the table. *Ouch.* Not a dream, then.

But previous experience had hardwired her to be wary of any kind of 'persuasion'.

She said, 'If I refuse what happens?'

Massimo took a drink of water and shook his head, 'Absolutely nothing. Things proceed as normal. You are under no obligation to agree to this. I realise that it's asking you to blur the boundaries of our work relationship. I don't want you to feel uncomfortable. You don't have to answer now, Carrie. Think about it and let me know later.'

Something in her eased. She was an expert in reading passive aggression and aggressive aggression, and she perceived nothing here. Massimo was telling the truth. He really was just looking for an easy option in something he considered irksome.

But nevertheless her urge to self-protect was stronger than her instinct that she could trust him.

'I'm sorry but I can't agree to do this. I don't need to think about it.'

Immediately a knot of regret clutched at her gut. She pushed it down.

His expression didn't falter. 'If that's your final decision then I accept it.'

His gaze was steady. Dark. All-encompassing. They were outside on the terrace but she felt she needed air.

She stood up, 'I think I'll take my break now, if that's all right, s—' She'd been about to say, *sir,* but stopped herself.

'Of course—take all the time you need. I have to go

into the office for the rest of the day, and I'll be eating out this evening.'

Carrie left the lunch table with her half-eaten plate of food and went inside. There was a housemaid who came every day—a friendly young woman. She was in the kitchen now, and Carrie instructed her to clean up once Massimo had finished his lunch, and to make sure the chef knew that he was dining out this evening.

Then she made her way straight down to ground level and stepped outside, where she was met with a wall of still, humid air. Not the clear, refreshing oxygen she needed so she could try and wrap her brain around what Massimo had just asked of her. And her answer. Which had been met with equanimity.

She bought an iced tea from a nearby coffee shop and made her way over to Central Park, looking for even the smallest of breezes under the shade of the massive trees. She sat on a bench and watched people go by, sipping her drink.

A pair of young lovers, hand in hand, clearly besotted, caught her attention. Her heart spasmed. Growing up with her mother's stoicism after being dumped so comprehensively, Carrie had always prided herself on not having any illusions when it came to love and fairy tales of happy endings. But when she'd been vulnerable, and her husband had used all his manipulative charm to seduce her, she'd allowed herself to believe briefly that maybe it would be different for her.

But it hadn't been, and she should have known better. There was no such thing as romance. Only people who want to control and dominate others…take advantage of any vulnerability. There was no equality. Only power games. And she'd never be on the wrong side of that equation again.

She'd had to refuse Massimo, to see how he'd react. Like some kind of test. And because she'd sensed no passive aggression that might threaten to blow up at a later point she couldn't help but wonder if she'd over-reacted.

As if to mock her for her cynicism, the young lovers had stopped to kiss now, and it was sweet yet passionate. They were oblivious to voyeurs. Before she could deny it, Carrie felt a sense of yearning. An ache for something she'd told herself didn't exist. Maybe it did for some people, who weren't damaged or driven to manipulate and dominate.

Then a mother passed her, with a baby in a stroller, and an even bigger ache gripped Carrie right in her womb. She put a hand there unconsciously, as if that might dim the pain. That was when she realised that it wasn't sharp, as it had used to be. It was softer. Still there, but not so acute.

Time really was a healer. Such a cliché. But she couldn't deny feeling a sense of peace after four long years of hiding and licking her wounds.

Maybe, whispered a little voice, *just maybe it's time to stop hiding yourself away? Maybe it's time to live a little again?*

A tiny bud of something light unfurled inside her. Along with a frisson of electricity at the thought of being brave enough to accept Massimo's invitation.

If there was a way to start embracing life again, then surely standing beside Massimo, Lord Linden, had to be a pretty audacious place to start?

CHAPTER THREE

MASSIMO WAS DISTRACTED, and he'd been distracted all afternoon and evening. It wasn't every day that a woman turned him down. That *anyone* turned him down. He felt irritated with himself at the fact that it bothered him. Carrie was his housekeeper—clearly she was being professional and he should commend her for it.

If he'd been trying to test her she'd passed with flying colours. What he had asked of her was beyond the realms of regular service and he knew well that his motives weren't as straightforward as he'd led her to believe. He'd hoped that if she said yes, then she would lose whatever fascination she held for him.

More than fascination.

He shifted in his seat in the back of his car as it made its way through the night-time Manhattan traffic.

He'd just endured an interminable dinner where, as his peers had grown drunker and drunker, he'd found his mind wandering back to Carrie. The look of shock on her face earlier when he'd suggested eating together. The way she'd sat there so primly. The way she'd spoken to him, asking him things no one else ever had.

She intrigued him.

But perhaps she'd sensed his interest and her low-key and humble demeanour was an act.

A part she'd been playing for four years just to engage his interest?

The voice mocked his cynicism, but at the same time, considering the lengths some women had gone to to get his attention, it was not entirely beyond the realm of possibility.

But he couldn't deny that she'd first intrigued him four years ago, when she'd come to be interviewed for the position as his housekeeper. So it had been brewing under the surface for a long time.

Massimo tried to be rational about this irritating growing desire for a woman who was plainly out of bounds—and for good reason. Apart from anything else, it went against all his tenets to pursue a woman like Carrie Taylor.

He only pursued women who knew how to play the game and who were like him—from a world that had calcified them into something hard and cynical.

He only pursued women who were happy with one night. Because he never wanted anything more. And he certainly had no desire for any kind of longevity.

He scowled at himself as the car pulled up outside his apartment building. How had he somehow meandered to *these* thoughts?

Carrie Taylor, his aggravating housekeeper. That was how. As he stepped out of the car and went inside he sent up silent thanks for her refusal to accede to his wishes. She had done them both a favour. Tomorrow he would instruct his assistant to set up that model as his date.

That intention lasted as he arrived in the apartment and loosened his tie. It lasted as he went into the kitchen, looking for something more substantial to eat than the risible air and leaves they'd been served at dinner. It lasted right up until a familiar voice came from behind him.

'There's some leftover steak. I could make you a sandwich if you like?'

Massimo stopped and turned around. And all his good intentions dissolved in a flash of heat. And lust.

Carrie was out of her uniform and wearing something soft and slouchy…a sweatshirt and leggings. But far more incendiary than that, her hair was down. He'd never seen her hair down. In four years.

It was far wilder than he would have expected. And longer. Flowing loose and wavy over her shoulders and down her back. He suspected some would say it was unfashionably long, and it certainly wasn't styled, but seeing it down like this made him feel like a voyeur from another era. It felt ridiculously intimate, and for the first time in a long time he was speechless.

She gestured to herself, looking embarrassed, 'Sorry, I'm off duty. I hope you don't mind. I know you don't normally see me like this.'

Massimo shook his head. 'No, not at all.'

Had she mentioned food? His head felt foggy. He struggled to remember. All he knew was that he didn't want her to leave.

He said, 'Did you say a sandwich? That would be amazing. Thank you.'

He slipped off his jacket and saw how her eyes followed his action. Her cheeks went pink. Massimo's blood was on fire.

She came into the kitchen, the lights glinting off her bright hair. She was wearing socks. Her legs were long and shapely. The soft clothes clung to her body, showcasing womanly curves. She'd put on weight since she'd started working for him and it suited her. She'd been so delicate in those earlier days…she'd looked as if a puff of wind would blow her over.

The sweatshirt slipped off one shoulder and Massimo had an almost overwhelming urge to go over, pull her hair aside and press his mouth there. She pulled it back up and he gritted his jaw.

He moved around to the other side of the island, suddenly aware of his body's response.

She was efficient in her movements, brisk, and she said over her shoulder, without making eye contact, 'If you'd like, I can bring it to you. it shouldn't take me long.'

A perverse devil inside Massimo made him say, 'No, it's okay. I'll wait here.'

He draped his jacket over a chair and went over to the fridge and pulled out a bottle of sparkling water. He took a glass off the shelf. Sat down on the other side of the island.

There was silence as Carrie busied herself taking out the steak to warm it up, along with some bread. After a while she said, 'They didn't feed you at dinner?'

'Oh, they fed us. It just didn't remotely resemble any nutritious food group. Or consist of calories, for that matter.'

Massimo thought he heard a sound like a stifled laugh, but he couldn't be sure.

'Did you have dinner here?' he asked.

She could have gone out, for all he knew—perhaps even on a date. He'd never used a dating app in his life, but he'd heard of them. Maybe Carrie had one on her phone...

'Yes, I had steak and salad.'

Massimo really didn't like his sense of satisfaction at hearing she hadn't gone out.

She turned around and deftly put the sandwich together, then arranged it on a plate along with some side salad.

She reached across the island and placed it in front of him. Massimo had to admit it looked and smelled delicious.

Before he could taste it, Carrie cleared her throat and said, 'Actually, I was hoping to catch you when you came in...to say something.'

'Of course.'

She looked nervous, avoiding his eye. Fingers plucking at a tea-towel. Then she seemed to muster her courage and looked at him. Once again he marvelled at how green her eyes were. Unusual...

Beautiful.

'I...um... I know that I refused your request that I join you at the event this week...and you've probably already asked someone else…' She trailed off here, as if waiting for him to interject.

Surprise kept Massimo's mouth shut.

She went on, 'But if you haven't asked anyone else, and you'd still like me to accompany you, then I will.'

A steady thrum of satisfaction beat through Massimo's body. A short while before he'd been telling himself he was pleased that she'd said no. But now he was even more pleased.

He said, 'I haven't asked anyone else yet, so…yes, I would like you to accompany me.'

Her mouth compressed. 'Like I said, I don't have anything suitable to wear… I can have a look on my lunchbreak, or after work…'

Massimo shook his head. It was already filling with visions of how she might look draped in silk and satin. Jewels glittering against her pale skin.

'Leave that to me. My assistant will be in touch to ensure you have all that you need.'

'Oh, okay…goodnight, sir.'

She turned to go and Massimo said softly from behind her, 'The name is Massimo.'

She turned around again, her face pink. 'Sorry, I forgot. Goodnight, Massimo.'

A lick of pure lust went straight to his groin at hearing his name on her tongue. He wanted to hear it over and over again. Begging him.

'Goodnight, Carrie.'

She turned and left. Her scent lingered on the air. Nothing expensive, but no less compelling. It was delicate and floral with an earthy undertone.

He looked at the steak sandwich. His appetite had fled, to be replaced by something far more carnal.

Carrie had never much indulged in fantasy. Not even as a child with a single mother, living in a council flat. The life she'd seen around her had been bleak and hard and she'd accepted her place in it.

She shook her head at herself, trying to dislodge the painful memories. But it was hard, because the present moment felt dangerously close to a fantasy she'd never allowed herself to have before. A fantasy of transformation. Of becoming someone else. Of being someone else. Someone far…sleeker. Shinier. Someone almost beautiful.

Her mother had been beautiful. Carrie had always recognised that. But her beauty had been dimmed and hidden under years of disappointment, loneliness and back-breaking work.

For the first time, as Carrie looked in the mirror, she thought she could catch a glimpse of what her mother might have looked like with a different life.

You're not your mother, whispered a little voice.

No, she wasn't. She was herself. And she was looking disbelievingly at a vision.

A team of people had arrived at Massimo's apartment earlier—stylists with racks of clothes, hairdressers, make-up artists…beauticians. She still blushed when she thought of how they'd attended to parts of her body that hadn't seen daylight for a long time.

They'd trimmed her hair, taking out some of the heavy weight before pulling it up into a kind of chignon.

They'd spent an hour on her face only to give her the effect of not wearing any make-up at all. Her eyes looked bigger, and very green. Cheeks dewy. Had her mouth always been so plump? Had they injected something into her lips without her even realising? She touched her mouth experimentally. It felt the same.

She was almost afraid to look at the dress. She barely even felt it on her, it was so light. Strapless. Black. Snug around her chest and waist and hips, before falling to the floor in soft folds, some of which were draped over her hip, giving an almost Grecian effect.

It was too low across her breasts. They looked...*provocative* to her eye. And yet she knew well that compared to the kind of thing some women wore at the events Massimo attended and hosted, this was positively discreet.

One part of her wanted to rip everything off, clean her face and jump into bed under the covers, but another part of her—a very fledgling part—felt excited at the thought of Massimo seeing her like this. Looking at her. Seeing her differently?

Her pulse throbbed. In her head a small voice was warning: *Danger! Danger!* But it was too late, because Massimo was coming to get her any minute now.

She tried to claw back some sense of reality before he came, telling herself that this was just a Cinderella moment. He would see how inferior she was next to all those other women tonight and he wouldn't ask her to accompany him again. Things would go back to normal and that was okay.

That was more than okay, she assured herself fiercely.

She took a deep breath. Tried to calm her pulse. This was a moment out of time. A moment to indulge in fantasy and then go back to the real world in approximately three hours. Massimo was ruthless about the time he spent at functions. In and out.

There was a knock on the door.

He was here.

Against Carrie's better efforts, all her attempts to keep her feet on the ground dissolved in a rush of nerves and heat. For a moment she felt light-headed. Tipping dangerously close to the edge of losing herself again... of allowing herself to dream of another life.

She took a deep breath. Calmed herself. She was not that girl any more. Any dreams she'd harboured had been well and truly shattered. She was a grown woman, and she knew exactly what was going on here.

Nothing much at all.

She called out, 'Come in,' but at the last moment couldn't turn around to face Massimo. Because she was too afraid to see the look on his face when he saw her and compared her to every other woman in his life.

When Massimo walked into the room Carrie had her back to him. The dress was strapless. The top of her back was bare, shoulders straight. Her skin was pale, almost pearlescent in the light. Her hair was swept up into a rough chignon and the line of her neck seemed to him to be incredibly delicate. Vulnerable.

For a heart-stopping moment Massimo didn't want her to turn around. He had a superstitious notion that once she did everything would change. That he'd embarked on something that was already leaving his control.

But it was too late. She was turning around, and he couldn't stop her, and she was…breathtaking. Literally. Like a gem revealed after layers of dust had been brushed away.

His first thought was, *Why has she hidden herself away?* His second thought was, *I want her.* It beat through him like a drum. Heavy and insistent.

The dress was black and form-fitting, a classic design. The bodice was cut low over her chest and clung lovingly to the fullness of her breasts, held up by some feat of engineering that Massimo could only guess at.

His gaze continued down to where the material defined her small waist and then gathered and draped over her hips and thighs before falling in long loose folds to her feet.

It was all at once classically elegant and indecently sexy.

Incredibly, he managed to drag his gaze back up and find his voice. 'You look…beautiful.'

'I feel a little exposed.'

He looked at her. High cheekbones. Delicate jaw, but strong. She was pink in the face. Her eyes looked very green, as if they too had been dulled until this moment. She wore minimal make-up because she evidently didn't need it. A slick of flesh-coloured lipstick. Slightly smoky eyes.

'Your dress is fine, believe me.'

'If you say so… I've never been to anything like this before.'

And they hadn't even left his apartment yet.

Massimo's conscience pricked. He ignored it. There was no way he could turn back now. A floodgate had been opened and for the first time in his life he felt like throwing caution to the wind.

He walked towards her and held out the box he was holding in his hands. He'd almost forgotten.

She looked from it to him, suddenly wary. 'What's this?'

'An embellishment.'

Not that she needed it.

She took a step towards him, and Massimo gritted his teeth as her scent tickled his nostrils. Light, but with those subtle undertones of something much more potent. Like her…with hidden depths.

He opened the box and she looked down. He could see the pink leach from her face. Not the reaction he would have expected when a woman laid eyes on an art deco diamond and emerald necklace from one of the world's most iconic jewellers.

'What is this?' She looked up at him.

Massimo lifted the necklace from the box and put the box down. He said, 'Turn around.'

She looked stricken. 'I can't wear that…it's too much.'

'I've been given strict instructions by the stylist that it's an integral piece of your ensemble. Plus, the jewellers who have loaned it to me will be at the event this evening.'

Some colour came back into her cheeks. 'It's on loan?'

'Yes. Now, turn around.'

Slowly, she did so, and Massimo reached over her head to place the necklace at her throat and close it behind her neck. His fingers brushed her skin and it felt warm and soft. Was it his imagination or did a little tremor go through her body?

He took his hands away. 'Okay, you can turn around again.'

She did so, her hands touching the necklace as if she was afraid it might fall off. She was avoiding his eye. His blood pulsed.

She was as aware of him as he was of her. She wanted him.

Except normally when he realised a woman wanted him he felt a sense of satisfaction. Now all he felt was intense hunger. The kind he hadn't felt in a long time. Raw and urgent.

'Carrie, look at me.'

Carrie really didn't want to look at Massimo. Her skin was still tingling from where his fingers had brushed against her. Her eyeline was on his bow-tie. Even in heels the top of her head only grazed his jaw. The necklace felt cold and heavy around her neck. No plastic gems here. Real emeralds and diamonds.

She'd seen Massimo dressed in a tuxedo a million times before, but it had never impacted on her the way it did this evening. Even his scent seemed stronger. More potent.

Boundaries and lines felt very blurry right now, standing here in front of her boss, dressed like someone who was not her—plain old Carrie Taylor, a girl who hadn't even done her A-levels, nothing but a humble housekeeper...

'Carrie?'

She forced the cacophony out of her head, took a deep breath and looked up. Everything about him should be signalling danger to her—he was so much bigger and stronger physically than her husband had been—but she felt no danger. Only intense excitement and anticipation.

Her heart skipped a beat when she registered the intensity in his dark gaze. She instantly felt self-conscious. As if she'd been caught playing dress-up.

She took a step back. 'If you've changed your mind it's okay, honestly. I don't mind.'

Massimo frowned. 'Why would I change my mind? You look stunning.'

Self-consciousness turned to awareness. Even though she knew he was only being polite. 'I think the team you provided could make anyone look presentable.'

'You're more than presentable, Carrie. You're beautiful.'

Her heart hitched again. Warning bells rang in her head. Memories of her husband...

'Carrie, you're so special. I want to protect you.'

She forced her brain to cool down and slow down. 'Thank you, but it's really not necessary to say things like that. It's not as if this is a real date.'

'I'll spare you the platitudes, then?' Massimo responded dryly.

Carrie just managed to stop herself from reminding him that she wasn't one of his usual lovers. *As if he needed reminding.*

He seemed to wait a moment for a response, and when she said nothing he said, 'My driver is waiting downstairs. We should go.'

Carrie welcomed the respite from his focus and let him lead her out of the apartment and down to the waiting car. They got into the back and it moved smoothly through the evening Manhattan traffic.

She looked out at the crowds of people. Some rushing home, some just strolling along, some lovers holding hands. And here she was, dressed in a gown she could never afford in her lifetime, sitting beside one of the world's most eligible bachelors, about to attend a glittering event. She was living out a fantasy she'd never even admitted to having.

'Don't worry, you'll be fine—just follow my lead.'

Carrie looked at Massimo, who glanced down at her hands in her lap, where she was gripping her clutch bag so tight her knuckles were white.

She realised how tense she was and took a breath, loosening her grip. 'I don't want to embarrass you.'

'You won't.'

She wasn't so sure about that. She felt certain that everyone would see her shortcomings and lack of credentials like a branded letter on her forehead.

As if he could hear her thoughts, Massimo said, 'You know, not everyone you'll meet will have been born with advantages. Some have made their livelihoods from nothing. Literally from living on the streets. Some of them had rough starts in life.'

Carrie's face flushed. She didn't want to come across as prejudiced. 'I know that…but if anything that makes people even more intimidating. To know the obstacles they've overcome to succeed…'

'Unlike someone like me?'

There was no edge to his tone, but Carrie thought of all the stories about his young life—unbelievably privileged, but also chaotic. Losing his parents so young. Then his brother. Did wealth and privilege make those things any easier to bear? She suspected not.

She smiled a small smile, 'I guess it's all relative. Everyone has obstacles.'

He looked at her for a long moment. She thought he was about to ask her something, but then the car was pulling to a stop outside the very grand entrance of a building. Flashing lights almost blinded Carrie before they'd even got out of the car. Her terror was instant. She went cold all over.

She didn't even notice Massimo taking her hand and tugging her from the car, standing up straight beside him. It was a barrage of lights. She was stunned.

'Just follow me. We don't need to stop.'

But as they walked along the red carpet all Carrie could hear was, 'Massimo! Over here!'

'Massimo who's your date?'

'Massimo!'

She tried to tug at his hand, to tell him he should stop and get his photo taken, but to her relief he didn't seem to be inclined to stop. And now they were through the doors and into the most opulent and beautiful foyer Carrie had ever seen.

Marbled floors…a domed and frescoed ceiling soaring far above their heads. Elaborate chandeliers with hundreds of tiny lights cast everything in a golden hue. Black-suited waiters moved among the gilded crowd, offering tall, delicate glasses of sparkling wine.

Massimo took two glasses and handed her one. She felt light-headed without even taking a sip. It was like the set of a Disney movie. Except it had come to life. There was a grand staircase in the middle of the space leading up to the next level, where more people mingled.

The acoustics were perfect, letting the strains of live classical music float through the chattering crowd without sounding discordant.

'Where are we?'

She hadn't realised she'd spoken out loud until Massimo said, 'One of Manhattan's oldest buildings. Newly renovated as an event space exclusively for charitable events.'

Carrie looked at Massimo as something occurred to her. 'You own this, don't you?'

'It's an acquisition I made, yes. It seemed prudent to have a space to host events.'

In spite of her lingering intimidation and terror Carrie's mouth twitched at the thought of simply acquiring what had to be one of New York's most expensive properties to make one's life easier. Massimo looked at her mouth, and then into her eyes. It sent all sorts of languid heat along her veins.

He asked, 'What is so funny?'

He had his hand on her elbow. A light touch, but it

burned. The twitch left her mouth. She shook her head. 'Nothing. It's just a lot…to take in.' She took a sip of wine to try and quell her nerves.

Massimo guided her to the stairs and they walked up. He greeted people with a nod here and there. Carrie couldn't help noticing the intense interest he drew. And her. She felt all the eyes on her. Could almost hear the whispers.

Who is she?

What on earth is someone like her doing here?

Carrie had thought she'd be totally cowed but strangely, with Massimo by her side, she felt her spine straightening and her head coming up. She felt the protection of his very solid presence beside her like a force-field.

When they reached the next level Carrie was glad they'd lingered in the reception foyer for a while, giving her time to prepare her for the grandeur that awaited: a ballroom bigger than any space she'd ever been in, in her life.

Massive French doors were open to terraces outside. The glittering crowd mingled under thousands of lights that seemed to be hung by invisible threads over their heads. Flowers and greenery bloomed all around them, giving the effect of a garden inside. A small orchestra played on a dais in one corner.

They weren't alone for long. People started to approach Massimo in a steady stream. Out of nowhere, one of Massimo's assistants that Carrie recognised materialised by his side, and she could hear him reminding Massimo of who people were before they got to him.

Massimo introduced her to everyone, and they were perfectly civil, but their eyes and their attention skated over her. She wasn't interesting to them. Certainly not recognisable. That suited her just fine.

She was fascinated with how Massimo expertly gave his full attention to everyone, getting what he wanted to know from them, or imparting some information, and then moved onto the next person. He had the effortless diplomacy of a statesman.

When they moved into the adjacent space a short time later, Carrie realised it was a dining room. Lots of circular tables with elaborate floral centrepieces. They were led to one near the front, where there was a small stage with a podium.

Food was served and it looked surprisingly hearty. Not what she would have expected at an event like this. She picked up her fork, suddenly realising she was starving, but when she looked around her she put it down again quickly, her face growing hot at her faux pas.

Massimo turned away from the man he'd been talking to on his other side. 'Something wrong?'

Carrie whispered, 'No one is eating.'

'And you're hungry?'

She looked at him. 'I haven't eaten since this morning.' It had taken most of the day to make her look presentable.

Massimo picked up his fork and speared a large morsel of food, putting it into his mouth. It was almost comical the way everyone else at the table suddenly followed suit.

He winked discreetly at Carrie.

She ate some food and instantly felt a little less light-headed. A woman near her leaned towards her. She was older, and she had a pleasant expression on her face—less frozen than most of the women she'd noticed.

'And what's your name, dear?'

Carrie's mouth went dry. Was she meant to make conversation with these people? With her less than re-fined accent?

But before she could answer Massimo was saying smoothly, 'My apologies, Dorothy, this is Carrie Taylor.'

The woman's eyes lit up. 'One of the Taylors from Long Island? Now which one are you, dear? One of John's daughters?'

Massimo put a discreet hand on Carrie's arm. He said, 'No, she's not related to those Taylors. She's from London—that's where we met.'

Where we met.

As if she really was with him. As if she wasn't just an employee doing him a favour that crossed several boundaries.

Carrie could feel an urge to give in to this fantasy that somehow she was a peer of Massimo's and they'd met at an event like this, but it was too much of a stretch for her. She'd had the life she'd had, and there was some comfort in knowing that she didn't regret it. It had made her who she was and she was proud of that.

The older woman's face immediately blanked, now that Carrie was no longer someone she could relate to. She turned away to the man on her right.

Massimo said, *sotto voce*, 'Don't mind Dorothy… she's old school. She only knows how to talk to people descended from the pilgrims on the *Mayflower*.'

Carrie stifled a giggle. Then Massimo's thigh touched hers under the table. It was fleeting, but it sent a shockwave of arousal through her body. The urge to giggle faded and her appetite fled. She left the rest of the food on her plate.

She *had* to control herself. She couldn't allow herself to believe that this was somehow real. She'd believed in a fantasy before, and the consequences had been tragic. She'd promised herself she'd never be so blind again.

The waiters discreetly cleared their plates. There was a tapping sound on a microphone and then a woman stood on the podium and spoke a few words, welcoming everyone, before she said, 'There's no point in my saying another word—I might as well hand it over to the man best qualified to tell us more about his vision for this space, Massimo Black, Lord Linden.'

There was thunderous applause and Massimo was striding onto the stage before Carrie had even registered that he was gone from her side.

He was mesmerising. He shushed the crowd with a self-deprecating expression and then not a sound could be heard except for his deep voice as he spoke with clear confidence. And Carrie wasn't even taking in half of what he was saying about wanting to create a space that would be solely available for charitable causes…wanting to give organisations no excuse not to raise funds.

'And to that end,' Massimo was saying now, 'I will cover the costs of every event held here for the first year...'

Applause broke out and Massimo put up a hand.

'But that's only if a certain threshold is met tonight with charitable donations. I like to ensure that people feel galvanised into raising as much money as possible.'

He smiled the smile of a shark, and it reminded Carrie for a moment of who he was.

The applause was mingled with wry chuckles and some good-natured heckles. Carrie heard someone from the table behind her saying, 'Typical Massimo Black—generous, but always with a ruthless edge.'

Massimo put his hands together. 'Thank you. Now, please enjoy the rest of the evening and start conceiving all the events you will host. I look forward to the invitations.'

He was a consummate diplomat. And he was the most intimidating and charismatic man in the room. And now he was stepping down from the stage and walking towards where Carrie sat, his eyes on her.

Along with everyone else. Wondering who on earth she was. Why on earth she was with him. But she didn't have time to worry about what everyone was thinking because she was so consumed by that dark gaze.

Massimo stopped beside her and held out his hand. 'Shall we?'

Carrie wanted to ask, *Shall we what?* But, aware of people looking and listening, she stood up and put her hand in his. Her skin broke into goosebumps as he led her away from the table and she noticed everyone else getting up. As if they'd been waiting for his signal.

They moved through the dining room to yet another glittering room. A ballroom. Soft lighting and lots of gilded mirrors made it seem as if it was shimmering.

Carrie couldn't help a little sigh of awe. If someone pinched her right now she was sure she'd wake up and not just be back in London, in her little suite of rooms in Massimo's house, but back on the council estate where she'd lived with her mother.

There was a different band in here, playing music that was smooth and slow. Rhythmic. Carrie only re-alised what was happening when Massimo stopped, drew her in front of him and pulled her close, putting one arm around her back and taking her other hand in his and moving it up close to his chest.

Dancing.

She stiffened. And then, when he started to move and she had no choice but to follow him, she darted a look at everyone else milling about the room around them.

'I can't dance,' she hissed.

A toxic memory inserted itself into her head—her husband smiling at her indulgently, but with an edge, saying, *'Bless you, Carrie, you just don't have any natural grace.'*

'Neither can I—I've been faking it for years,' Massimo said, pulling her out of the past and back to the terrifying present. 'Just follow my lead.'

Carrie had no choice but to do as he said, and she found that once the panic started to dissolve her feet were moving of their own volition, in some approximation of dancing.

His arms felt very secure.

She felt safe.

It was a rogue thought, flashing through her mind and going again before she could refute it.

Other people were dancing too. Laughing. Chatting. Carrie relaxed a little more into Massimo's embrace. She let the music wash over her…through her. She had to stop herself from moving even closer. She wanted to press her body against his. It made her tremble.

'You're doing great, Carrie.'

She looked up at him and couldn't look away.

Massimo nearly stopped dancing. Carrie's eyes were huge, and full of more expression than he could remember seeing in any woman's face. Usually what he saw was fawning. Guile. Calculation. Hard cynicism.

What he saw in Carrie's eyes was totally unguarded. Awe. Fear. *Desire.* His body thrummed with need. She felt like steel and silk in his arms. Incredibly strong but also vulnerable.

He couldn't take his gaze off her mouth. He wanted to cover it with his own. Brand her lips with a kiss so deep and carnal that she would be left in no doubt that he wanted her.

'I want you.' It came out of his mouth on a raw breath. He only realised he'd spoken out loud when Carrie stopped moving.

Her eyes widened with shock and her cheeks went pink. 'You…what?'

But she didn't wait for him to say anything. She pulled free of his embrace and pushed through the crowd.

Massimo cursed. What the hell was wrong with him? He followed her.

CHAPTER FOUR

CARRIE BLINDLY MADE her way through the crowd and off the dance floor to the closest escape route she could see. Open French doors leading out to a terrace. She needed air. Blood was thundering in her head.

The terrace was mercifully quiet. For once she didn't notice the city laid out before her, buildings soaring tall on either side.

Massimo's words reverberated in her head: *I want you... I want you...* Away from him now, though, she wondered if she'd misheard him. A different kind of heat crept into her face. Shame.

Did he overwhelm her so much that she'd conjured up the words that she wanted to hear?

'Carrie.'

He was behind her. Her skin prickled. She composed herself and turned around, forcing a breezy smile. 'Sorry, the heat got to me.'

I thought I heard you say you wanted me.

'I needed some air.'

She was avoiding his eye, fixing her gaze somewhere around his jaw. It was tight. A muscle popped.

He said, 'Look, I'm sorry about that.'

Reluctantly she looked at him. His face was in shadow. All angles and edges. 'Sorry about...?'

Sorry about wanting her, of course!

He grimaced. 'I was thinking it. I didn't realise I'd spoken out loud.'

Carrie's heart thumped. 'Thinking that...?'

'I want you.'

He'd said it again. She hadn't been dreaming or hallucinating. She felt trembly. She was glad the wall of the terrace was behind her, giving her some sense of support.

'I don't know what to say.'

Massimo came and stood next to her, facing out towards the city. Hands on the wall. 'You don't have to say anything. I've overstepped the mark.' He looked at her. 'You're under no obligation, Carrie. You can leave now if you wish. My driver will take you back to the apartment. I won't put you in this position again.'

He turned around and went back into the ballroom. Impossible to miss. He was soon accosted by an eager crowd.

Carrie knew he was giving her an opportunity to restore the boundaries of their relationship. To go back to how it had been. But something seismic had just happened. He'd told her he wanted her. He desired her.

Massimo Black, an earl and a lord, one of the world's most charismatic and enigmatic men, wanted *her*. Carrie Taylor. A woman who had seen and experienced the rougher edges of life since birth. A woman who had been brought low by her own vulnerability and hollowed out by grief.

Sometimes Carrie felt much older than her twenty-six years. She'd never really indulged in anything frivolous and just for her. She'd never had the luxury of being so selfish. She'd gone from grieving for her mother to embarking on a relationship that would dominate her life until tragedy finally ended it.

She'd never felt the range of sensations that Massimo could evoke with just a look or brief touch. Not even with her husband, a man she'd believed she loved.

Just now, in Massimo's arms... It was almost embarrassing how aware she'd been of every inch of her body. The way her breasts had felt heavy. Her gut tight with tension. And lower, between her legs, she'd felt achy with a longing she'd never experienced before.

Massimo was still standing in the crowd, towering above almost everyone else. He was surrounded by people. Women. Yet in that moment he cut a very lonely figure to Carrie. She felt no pity. What she did feel—shockingly—was a sense of possessiveness. Especially when one of the women put a hand on his arm to get his attention.

Acting on instinct, not thinking of what her actions might mean, Carrie walked through the crowd to Massimo. As if sensing her, he turned his head and saw her. She saw a flare in his eyes. A flare of heat. And... gratitude?

He put out a hand, dislodging the woman's fingers from his arm. Carrie took his hand, feeling ridiculously thrilled by the attention. He pulled her into his side, hand tight on her waist.

So this was what it felt like. To be chosen by Massimo. Like basking in the benevolent warmth of the sun, heat prickling along her veins.

He introduced Carrie to some more people but they all blurred into one at some point, and her cheeks hurt from smiling. Her feet were also killing her in the high heels.

Eventually he said, 'Ready?'

Carrie blinked and looked around. There was no one else waiting to talk to Massimo. The crowd had thinned out. Only a few people were left on the dance floor.

She thought of that word. *Ready*. Was she ready for whatever she'd tacitly put in motion by not leaving? Not in a million years. But she knew that she'd prefer to be here than back at the apartment feeling a sense of regret.

Carrie looked up at Massimo. She wanted to project cool confidence, but in that moment, under his penetrating gaze, her insides quivered.

'The truth is, I'm not sure.'

Massimo lifted her hand to his mouth and pressed his lips to her palm. A touch that felt shockingly intimate considering that up till now every physical interaction between them had been totally solicitous.

'Nothing will happen that you're not comfortable with, Carrie. I can promise you that.'

Something eased inside her. She hadn't expected Massimo to be so unapologetically direct. He wasn't trying to charm her, or flatter her, or guilt her into anything.

He led her from the room, saying goodbye to a few

people en route. His car and driver were waiting out-side. The evening was still and warm. It felt as if the world was holding its breath for something.

Carrie shook her head at herself. She was being ri-diculous. The car was moving now. She tried to pretend she was absorbed with what was happening outside the windows, but she was attuned to every tiny move Mas-simo made. His scent. The fact that he'd undone his bow-tie and the top button of his shirt. The fact that he lounged beside her, long legs sprawled out.

In contrast she felt incredibly uptight. Tense. Sud-denly wondering what on earth she was thinking. She couldn't possibly do this. What had she even agreed to do? Sleep with Massimo? Panic started to rise. If they slept together she'd lose her job! She really hadn't thought this through at all.

She turned to Massimo—and promptly forgot what she was going to say. They were pulling up outside his building now. He took her hand again and led her inside. To his private elevator. He and the concierge exchanged words. She didn't even take it in. His hand was tight on hers, as if he sensed her vacillating turmoil.

The elevator ascended. Doors opened. Carrie's breath was coming short and fast. If she wasn't careful she'd hyperventilate. She took a deep breath. She had noth-ing to fear here. Massimo wouldn't force her...

A sliver of cold went down her back. But how did she know that for sure? She'd witnessed how a man could turn into something else entirely.

Massimo let her hand go to enter the apartment and Carrie put some distance between them. She put her bag down on a table. The lights were low. She had her back to Massimo, but she sensed he wasn't coming closer.

She turned around. He was near the door. Jacket open. Face cast in shadow. But she could still see its hard angles. The sensual curve of his mouth.

'Carrie…?'

She bit her lip and then said, 'Look… I don't want to be a tease…but I'm not sure this is such a good idea.'

He shook his head. 'You're not being a tease. No woman is ever a tease, Carrie.'

Another knot inside her eased. 'We haven't really spoken about what this is…'

He stepped forward, out of the shadows. She could see his face now. It held a stark expression she'd never noticed before.

He said, 'It's desire. Mutual desire.'

'But how…? Why now?'

'I think it was always inevitable…we just didn't acknowledge it till now. The first day I met you I noticed you, Carrie. But I managed to push it away…ignore it. Until I couldn't any more.'

To know that he had felt a similar sense of awareness from day one made something shift inside Carrie. Gave her a sense of confidence. Nevertheless, she felt compelled to be the voice of reason when it felt as if everything she knew was going up in flames around her.

She shook her head faintly. 'I don't know if this is really a good idea…'

Massimo took another step closer. Now he looked serious. 'You're probably right.'

Carrie's stomach dropped. And that told her all she

needed to know about how she really felt about the po-
tential consequences.

'But…' she said, and stopped, not wanting to sound
too desperate. She forced a light tone into her voice,
'We're both adults, it's not as if I'm under any illusions
about what this would be…'

Massimo frowned. 'What do you mean?'

Now Carrie felt self-conscious. 'I know that it would
be one night only. You don't ever do more than one
night…with a woman.'

Massimo's face had turned to stone. Completely ex-
pressionless. Then he said, 'You're right. I don't.'

'So this would be no different.'

After a beat he said, 'No, it wouldn't.'

Carrie didn't like the little twist near her heart when
she heard that, but it was important to let him know
that she wasn't some starry-eyed fool who didn't know
the score.

'Okay, then.'

Massimo's expression relaxed. 'Okay, then?'

Carrie's heart thumped. She felt gauche. Embarrassed by the fact that she didn't know how to be sultry. Seductive.

Massimo seemed to take pity on her. He said, 'Turn
around.'

She did so, relieved to escape that gaze. She could
see Massimo's tall figure reflected in the window across
the room. She could feel him come closer behind her
and shivered a little.

'Cold?' he asked.

She shook her head.

He knew that she wasn't shivering from the cold. He was probably enjoying watching her less than sophisticated reaction. She would have scowled, but he moved even closer, and now she could feel the heat from his body licking around her.

She quivered with anticipation. She had no idea what he was going to do, where he was going to touch her. But then she felt him touch her hair, starting to take the pins out. Gently.

Bit by bit, the mass of her hair came undone and tumbled around her shoulders. Then Massimo put his hands in her hair and massaged her scalp. Carrie's eyes closed. She didn't know what she'd been expecting but it hadn't been this, and it felt good enough to turn her bones to rubber.

'Your hair...' Massimo said from behind her. 'I never expected your hair to be like this. You never leave it down.'

Carrie struggled to wrap her tongue around words. 'Not at work, no.'

He put his hands on her shoulders and slowly turned her around. She felt light-headed. Dreamy, but wide awake at the same time. Languorous, but energised.

'Do you mind if I take off my shoes?' she asked.

'Let me.'

Before she could stop him Massimo was down at her feet, reaching under the silken folds of her dress. She lifted her foot and he slipped off one shoe, then the other. It dropped her a few inches, but he was still at her feet. His hand was around her ankle. He looked up at her and her throat went dry at the sight of this beautiful man, kneeling at her feet.

Never taking his eyes off hers, he moved his hand up from her ankle, around her calf and to her knee. She had to put a hand on his shoulder to stay steady.

His hand moved up the back of her thigh.

Her skin tightened all over and a sharp arrowing of need went straight between her legs.

His fingers brushed against the lace of her underwear.

To her dismay and relief, Massimo took his hand away and stood up, letting her dress fall. He didn't touch her.

For a split-second Carrie wondered if he'd just realised he was making a terrible mistake. But then he said, 'Carrie, if you want to stop, just say the word and I'll stop. It doesn't matter at what point.'

Carrie had a very unwelcome flashback to her husband, saying nastily, *At some point men can't stop. It's physically impossible. So don't put me in that position again. It's your fault.*

She went cold.

Massimo put a hand on her arm. 'Carrie? What is it?'

She shook her head. She did not want those memories here. This was not the place for them. This was the present and her new future opening up. She wouldn't go back to that dark place.

She looked up at Massimo, lifted her chin. 'I'm not an innocent. I was married…but it's been a while.'

Massimo frowned slightly. 'Your husband…was he…?'

'I don't want to talk about him.' Carrie cut him off sharply.

He seemed to accept that. 'We'll take it slow…okay?'

Carrie nodded. Glad that she'd at least warned him not to expect fireworks. He put a finger under her chin and his head dipped towards hers. A burst of nerves suddenly assailed her.

She blurted out, 'You know, I'm really not very good at…this.'

Massimo paused inches from her mouth. His mouth quirked. 'Let me be the judge of that.'

Carrie was about to say, *That's what I'm afraid of,* but her words were swallowed by Massimo's mouth settling over hers, stealing her breath and every conscious thought in her head.

It wasn't a kiss. It was a claiming. It was elemental. Carrie opened her mouth unconsciously, allowing Massimo access. Allowing him to delve deep and find all her secrets, feel her reticence. Her inexperience.

But she couldn't worry about any of that now. She was acting on instinct. An instinct as old as time. An ancient dance. She was freed of all concerns. There was only here and now and the hot intensity entwining her with this man.

His hands were in her hair, holding her so that he could explore even deeper, and then he was tipping her face up so that he could trail his lips along her jaw and down along her neck to her shoulder.

The dress felt too tight around her breasts. She couldn't breathe. She wanted to break free of every constriction. Without even commanding her hands to do it, she was pushing Massimo's jacket off his shoulders and down his arms, pulling away his tie and throwing it aside, opening his shirt to reveal his chest, broad and magnificent. Mouth-wateringly masculine and hard-muscled.

She'd never experienced such a carnal feeling before. This man was hers and she wanted him. Any insecurities were burned to ash by the strength of her desire.

For a moment Massimo pulled back, and Carrie looked up at him, breathing harshly. Her hands were on his chest. She was marvelling at his heat and perfection. Her mouth felt swollen. Her heart was pumping so hard she could almost hear it.

Massimo looked down at her, his shirt half on, half off, hair mussed. Eyes burning.

He reached out and cupped her jaw and said, almost as if to himself, 'Who *are* you?'

Massimo was fairly certain he'd never met this woman before. Her hair was a wild tangle around her bare shoulders. Cheeks slashed with colour. Eyes huge and glowing like two jewels. Mouth a lush, plump invitation to keep kissing her and never stop.

Carrie swallowed. 'I'm just me…no one special.'

Everything in Massimo rejected that. She was temptation incarnate. She was fascinating. And he wanted her with a hunger he couldn't ever remember experiencing before.

He caught one of her hands and led her out of the reception area and through the apartment to the elevator. Inside, he put her apart from him and watched her as it ascended the short distance. He knew that if he so much as touched her now he wouldn't stop and they'd make love right there.

He thought for a second of what she'd said—that she wasn't innocent, she'd been married, and how she'd cut off his attempt to ask her about her husband.

It occurred to him that she'd cut him off because she couldn't bear to talk about him—because it pained her to talk about him. Because she'd loved him.

That thought shouldn't affect Massimo, but it did. Like a little sharp burr under his skin. He knew the awful pain of losing someone you loved, and the thought that she'd loved someone that much sent something dark and incomprehensible through him.

Before he could try and figure it out, the doors of the elevator opened. He welcomed the distraction, took Carrie's hand and led her, barefoot, into his bedroom.

She stalled. He looked at her.

She said, 'You don't usually…you know…in your own bedroom.'

No. He didn't. He usually avoided bringing his lovers into his personal space. But nothing was usual about this situation. He found he didn't really care that Carrie was in his bedroom. She already inhabited his personal space, so maybe that was what made it different? He certainly wasn't prepared to analyse it right now. He just wanted her.

'We can go to your bedroom if that's what you'd prefer?'

She shook her head and her hair slipped down over her shoulders, resting close to the swells of her breasts. 'No, it's fine…it doesn't matter. I don't know why I even said that.'

* * *

Carrie was kicking herself.

Just stop talking!

As if she needed to *remind* Massimo that this was not his usual modus operandi!

Her hand was still in his. He led her over to the bed. The room was cast in shadows and she was grateful. She felt far too exposed.

He said, 'Turn around.'

She obeyed, with a little shiver. What was it about him telling her to turn around? The fact that she didn't know what he was going to do? The fact that she was prepared to trust him to such an extent was seismic, but she did. It was instinctual and bone-deep. Perhaps four years of living alongside this man and observing him had given her more of an insight into him than she'd realised.

His fingers touched the top of her back as he moved her hair to one side, over one shoulder. Deftly he undid the necklace and lifted it from her neck, putting it down on the bedside table. Then his fingers trailed down the centre of her back to where the dress's zip started.

He started to pull it down and Carrie's breath grew shorter and sharper. She wasn't wearing a bra because the dress had enough support. It loosened around her chest and fell away as Massimo pulled the zip all the way down to just above her buttocks. With a little tug he pulled it over her hips, and it fell to the ground around her feet in a pool of satin. Now she was naked except for her very flimsy underwear.

'Carrie...'

She slowly turned around, her arms over her breasts in a self-conscious gesture. Massimo gently pulled them down and she heard his harsh intake of breath. She was too afraid to look at him. Not sure what she might see.

He reached out and traced the curve of one breast. Her nipples puckered into hard nubs. She had to bite her lip.

He said, 'You are…more than anything I could have imagined…'

Carrie couldn't quite fathom that he'd actually said that to her. But before she could let herself be overwhelmed by everything that was happening she reached for his shirt and pulled it all the way off and down.

He was now bare-chested, and he was beautiful. Powerful. Awesome. She reached out and put her hands on him again, spreading her fingers wide as if she could try and encompass every gleaming inch of flesh. He felt like steel underneath her palms.

She moved her hands down, emboldened by the way he was just letting her explore him. Trailed her fingers over the ridges of his abdominals. And then down to his lean waist. Not an ounce of excess flesh.

But then her attention snagged on his trousers. Belt buckle. She looked up and almost lost her nerve. She'd never seen such a stark expression on his face. All expression had leached away to be replaced with what she could only recognise as what she was feeling herself.

Need.

She couldn't move. She was transfixed. She heard rather than saw Massimo undo his belt, and then the sound of a button popping, the zip being lowered. Trousers dropping to the floor.

Mouth dry, Carrie looked down—and her mind blanked at the sight of Massimo's aroused body. He wrapped a hand around himself, as if he had to try and contain it.

'Get on the bed, Carrie.'

She half fell, half climbed onto the bed. Landing on her back, she looked up at Massimo, who seemed to have assumed the proportions of a mythic god. It was as if the world outside had fallen away completely and now they were in some parallel world, where nothing mattered except this man, this room and this moment.

Massimo came and rested over Carrie on both arms, muscles bunching. He bent his head and kissed her. This time it was slow and thorough. An exploration. When his tongue thrust deep it was a promise of what was to come. Between her legs she grew hot and damp…her body readying for its mate.

Massimo pulled back, as if she'd spoken that incendiary thought out loud. She looked up at him. But all he said was, 'Touch me, Carrie.'

She put her hands on him, running her palms down over his narrow hips and around to his buttocks, full and firm. One of his knees was between her legs, and with his hands he gently parted her thighs so they fell apart, opening her up to him.

Her avid gaze went to his erection. She'd never thought of that part of a man's body as particularly beautiful before. But Massimo's was. Long and thick and hard. Veins along the shaft. A thicket of dark hair at the base. Unashamedly masculine. Vital.

Unable to stop herself, she reached out and encircled him, shocked at how vulnerable he felt in her hand, yet strong. Silk over steel. He pulsed against her. A bead of moisture appeared at the tip.

She heard a small groan and wondered if it had been her or him. But then she did groan, as she felt his hand cup her between her legs. The flimsy lace was no barrier to the heat of his hand. His fingers tugged it to one side and he explored her, seeking and finding the heart of her that hadn't been touched in so long. That hadn't ever ached to be touched like this.

Sex had always felt cold to her. Tight. Uncomfortable. This was the direct opposite. She was on fire, pliable. Melting. Expanding. Opening.

Her back arched when Massimo thrust two fingers inside her. Her body was already clasping them, wanting more.

He said something guttural, and then, 'You're so responsive…'

Faint echoes of the past rang bells, reminding Carrie that once she'd been told the exact opposite. A voice sneering at her, *'You just lie there like a dead fish.'*

But the past melted away and she pushed it even further back, as Massimo's fingers moved in and out of her. Her hand tightened on him in a reflex response. He muttered a curse and took her hand away. She looked at him, feeling feverish, her hips circling in response to his hand between her legs. She barely recognised herself. Wanton. Fluid.

He took his hand away and left her for a moment. She heard him say something about protection and put an arm across her face. She hadn't even thought of it—that was how intoxicated she was.

He came back, rolling a sheath onto his body, totally unselfconscious. He moved between her legs, pushing them even wider, and with a quick economical movement ripped her underwear and threw it aside.

'I'll buy you new ones.'

Carrie couldn't care less. She was ravenous. She welcomed Massimo between her legs. Revelled in the way he took himself in his hand again and held the tip of his body against her hot, weeping flesh before pushing in, just a little. Just the swollen head. She sucked in a breath—not at the invasion but because it felt so *right*. As if something had been missing and was now slotting home.

'Okay?' he asked.

She couldn't speak. She could only nod and put her hands on his hips.

He sank deeper, and the stretch bordered on being painful, but then it bloomed into pleasure. He started to move in and out in slow, leisurely movements, letting her get used to the sensation, letting her body adapt to his.

Carrie bit her lip as the tension grew at her core, stoked and heightened by the way Massimo's body moved in a remorseless rhythm. She could feel perspiration on her own skin and see the sheen of moisture on Massimo's.

It was so earthy. So raw. She'd never known it

could be so base. Instinctively seeking relief, Carrie wrapped her legs around Massimo's waist and he slid even deeper. He came down on top of her, chest crushing her breasts, powerful buttocks moving faster now, one of his hands on her thigh, holding it against him.

She was trembling. Searching for something just of out of reach.

'That's it…come apart for me, Carrie.'

He put his mouth to her neck and bit her gently. She wanted him to bite harder. He palmed her breast and brought it to his mouth, sucking her nipple deep. She cried out, every atom of her being begging for release.

Massimo took his mouth from her breast and put a hand between them, where their bodies were joined. He touched her there and it sent shockwaves through her entire body. Shockwaves followed by an explosion of pleasure so exquisite that it bordered on being painful.

She was barely aware of Massimo's big body going still before jerking against her as he found his own release. She was undone. Torn apart and unable to piece together the sequence of events that had led to this seismic moment of pure and unadulterated bliss.

All she knew was that she'd never felt so at peace or so replete. So safe.

Silence settled over them. They were both breathing heavily. Their bodies were still joined and Carrie didn't want to let go of Massimo. She relished the sense of his heavy body on hers…in hers. Such a carnal thing. She'd be shocked at herself if she could drum up an ounce of sanity.

But slowly he moved, extricating himself.

Carrie felt a sense of loss and regret.

That was it. They'd never do this again.

But with the aftershocks of pleasure still moving through her body Carrie thought that maybe it was greedy to want to experience such transcendence again.

Emotion gripped her before she could stop it. Massimo had just restored something massive to her. The revelation that she was not cold, nor incapable of pleasure. Ever since her marriage, and in spite of knowing better, she'd always harboured a secret fear that she wouldn't ever feel sexually desirable or experience the kind of pleasure people talked about.

What she'd just experienced had exploded those fears apart. For ever.

Massimo lay still beside her. She was afraid to look at him, suddenly shy. A delicious lethargy was taking over her blood and bones, but she couldn't stop herself from saying, in a slightly hoarse voice, 'I never knew it could be so…'

Carrie's voice trailed off. But there was an answering thought in Massimo's head.

Neither did I.

He'd been having sex for years. Since well before he should have. And in all that time his first experience still stood out as being the moment that had blown his mind. Thanks to a very experienced older lover who had promptly dumped him once she'd taken the innocence of the legendary Linden heir. One of Massimo's first lessons in reality.

Since that first time sex had been pleasurable, yes, but never transcendent.

What had happened just now...*had* been transcendent. And he couldn't understand it.

From the moment he'd started to undress Carrie his brain had fused with white heat, and it was only returning to some semblance of normality now.

He felt drunk. Drunk on an overload of pleasure.

He turned his head and looked at her. She was asleep, curled on one side, facing him. Hair spread in a tangle around her head and on the pillow. Hands up under her chin in a curiously childlike gesture.

But the shape of her mouth, still swollen from his kisses, mitigated any childish gesture and was a reminder of how adult she was.

Massimo didn't have transcendent sex. He didn't *need* transcendent sex. He didn't need to transcend anything. That was why the Linden family fortune was still intact. Growing. Thriving. Precisely because, unlike his parents and his brother, he kept his feet firmly on the ground.

He'd never had the luxury of that kind of self-indulgence. From an early age he'd always known that he had to be the one to keep a clear head.

A memory came back out of nowhere. The housekeeper from Linden Hall—one of the few people in Massimo's life who had been a consistent benevolent presence. During one particularly chaotic party weekend at the hall he and his brother had been in the kitchen. She'd taken him aside and said, 'You don't have to live like this, Massimo. One day this will all pass to you and it'll be yours to keep. You can do things differently.'

Massimo could remember looking at his brother, who'd only been about ten, playing with toy cars on the other side of the kitchen while loud music still thumped upstairs. He'd seen his brother stop playing and look up with a yearning expression on his face, and he could remember vowing in that moment never to disrespect his legacy. To protect his brother from the excesses of their parents.

He'd managed to keep one promise at least.

A familiar hollow ache made his chest tight.

He pushed the memories aside.

Not now.

He looked at the woman beside him. For the first time in his life he wanted more than just a transitory meaningless encounter that left him momentarily satisfied but dissatisfied again within hours. He knew that he wouldn't feel dissatisfied after this. He would feel even hungrier. It was already building inside him— the clawing urge to join his body with hers again and seek oblivion.

He'd never wanted that with another woman. He'd always been happy to walk away.

Maybe this was what his parents and his brother had chased? This pull of pure pleasure? Maybe now it was his turn to indulge?

Carrie stirred on the bed. She opened her eyes a crack. Then a little more. She looked deliciously tousled. Sleepy. *Sexy*. Massimo sat back against the pillow. His body was already stirring. Again.

She came up on one elbow. She looked shy. 'We're still in your room…'

'You're very fixated on where we are.'

This was new territory for Massimo. Lingering in bed with a lover. But he found that his desire for Carrie was drowning out any concerns he should be heeding.

She pulled the sheet up over her body. He wanted to pull it back down. Put her on her back. Slide between her legs again. He gritted his jaw.

'I can go to my own room…' she said.

'Do you want to go to your own room?'

'Maybe I…should?'

'That's not answering my question.'

A flare of something made her eyes glow bright green. A flash of the personality that she usually hid. Massimo found it mesmerising.

She sat up, pulling the sheet over her chest. 'You don't do this.'

'As you keep telling me.'

'Are you saying you want me to stay?'

Massimo's gut clenched.

You really don't do this, prompted a little voice.

But he ignored it. 'I want you again.'

'I—' She stopped. Her cheeks flushed.

A sound like a giggle came out of her mouth and she put her hand up, embarrassed. Then she took it down. She was serious. And shy. An intoxicating combination.

She said, 'I want you too.'

Desire surged. Massimo reached out and lazily flicked the sheet away from her body. 'Then we won't be needing this, will we?'

CHAPTER FIVE

WHEN CARRIE WOKE up she was totally disorientated and still drowsy. It was bright outside. She wasn't in her own room. Her body had never felt so heavy. Or so tender. Especially between her legs…

She was fully awake in an instant. The bed beside her was empty. She sat up, holding the sheet to her chest. Someone had pulled it over her. *Massimo.*

Carrie had no idea what time it was, and she had that awful stomach-swooping sensation of having overslept. There was no sound at all. The en suite bathroom was empty but there was still a hint of steam in the air, as if it had been used not that long ago.

She spotted her dress, carefully laid over the back of a chair, and groaned when she recalled Massimo ripping off her underwear. She gingerly got out of the bed and found a robe hanging on the back of the bathroom door. It was still warm. Instant heat flooded Carrie's veins and she had to resist the urge to bury her nose in the fabric.

She saw the glittering necklace on the bedside table but couldn't see her underwear anywhere, so she gathered up the dress and shoes and crept out of the bedroom, using the stairs to go to her own room on the lower level.

Once in her room, she shucked off the robe and dived into the shower, turning the water to hot. She closed her eyes and lifted her face to the spray—but suddenly she was inundated with a slew of X-rated images from the previous night.

The second time they'd made love Massimo had almost forgotten to use protection and had thrust inside her before he'd remembered, with a curse. The thought that she could enflame such a man was seriously intoxicating. She had to put her hands on the wall of the shower, suddenly feeling unsteady at the memory of such passion.

The significance of what had happened hit her again. The fact that one night with Massimo had shown her in no uncertain terms that she was a woman capable of feeling intense pleasure and—she blushed—giving it. If Massimo's reaction had been anything to go by…

But it was over now. One night. Massimo never deviated in that practice.

She went cold in spite of the hot spray.

The thought of never again experiencing the sublime rapture of last night sent a skewer of pain through Carrie's gut. Then she felt disgusted with herself. She wasn't like the lovers she'd seen over the years with desperation in their eyes. She knew better.

She got out of the shower and briskly dried her hair, tied it back and put on her work clothes. She needed armour.

She went to the kitchen and the chef was there. Carrie felt as if she was branded with a scarlet letter on her forehead—H for Harlot—but he just said, 'Morning, Carrie, having some breakfast?'

She shook her head. She had no appetite. Not until she'd seen Massimo and got over that first hurdle. 'No thanks, is Lord—I mean, Mr Black, here?'

The chef indicated with his head. 'In the dining room.'

Carrie took a deep breath and straightened her shirt. She was wearing trousers and flat shoes. Cool, clean, crisp. Professional.

When she went in, Massimo was hidden behind a newspaper. She cleared her throat. He lowered the paper and she felt a wash of heat go out to every extremity from her core. He looked...amazing. Clean-shaven. Hair still a little damp.

He put the paper down, his eyes flicking over her clothes. 'Good morning.'

Carrie was almost struck dumb. 'I... Good morning...can I get you anything?'

'What's going on?'

'What do you mean?'

His hand indicated her clothes. 'You're dressed for work.'

'Of course I am. How else would I be dressed?'

Massimo reached over and pulled out a chair. 'Sit down...have some breakfast.'

'But I don't ever eat breakfast with you.'

'You do now.'

Carrie sat down, bemused. She'd expected Massimo

to be professional, business as usual. Brisk. But he was looking at her with a light in his eyes that didn't make her think of being brisk *or* professional.

'Coffee?'

Carrie blinked. Massimo was holding up a pot. Her boss was offering her coffee. 'Yes, please.'

He poured her a fragrant cup. Then he held up a plate of pastries. She took a croissant.

Suddenly she blurted out, 'This feels wrong. I shouldn't be here…like this.'

'Like what?'

Carrie felt a spurt of irritation at the way he was behaving so obtusely. 'Like a guest.'

The corner of Massimo's mouth twitched. 'I think we burned any such formalities to the ground last night.'

Mindful of the chef, not too far away, Carrie hissed, 'But you don't *do* this.'

Massimo rolled his eyes. 'This again…'

Carrie sat back. 'You don't have breakfast with them the morning after.'

Massimo took a sip of his own coffee, unconcerned. 'That's *them*. This is you—and now.'

Carrie's heart thumped. A little rogue inside her made her say, 'You're saying I'm different?'

His gaze sharpened on her. 'This whole situation is different. But I'm not offering anything more, Carrie. I made that decision a long time ago, and nothing and no one will convince me to change my mind. Let me be very clear: this lasts for as long as it lasts and then it will be over. I have no intention of making a long-term commitment to anyone.'

Why? The word hovered on Carrie's tongue, but anyone with an ounce of intelligence would be able to deduce from this man's well-documented history why he might be averse to making any long-term commitment. Not to mention whatever other personal reasons he had.

And in many ways—albeit for completely different reasons—she felt the same. She too had vowed never again to enter into a union that might destroy her.

Then she frowned when what he'd said fully sank in. *'This lasts for as long as it lasts.'*

Carefully, she asked, 'Are you saying that this…isn't it?'

Massimo sat back in his chair. 'I'm due to go to Brazil for the next few weeks. Rio de Janeiro. I have a conference to attend and then I was going to take a break.'

'I saw that on your schedule.'

She was due to go back to London when he was in South America.

'I want you to come with me.'

Carrie would have choked if there had been anything in her mouth

'You want me to come with you?' she repeated.

He nodded.

'As your housekeeper?'

He shook his head. 'No, as my lover.'

Carrie went very still. But inside she didn't feel still. She felt so many things she couldn't begin to decipher them. Confusion, excitement, trepidation. *Relief.* He still wanted her. She would experience the sublime again.

You'll lose yourself, pointed out a fearful voice.

'I don't think that's such a good idea.'

Carrie wasn't sure how she was managing to sound so cool and assured when she was still reeling and her insides were knotting and fizzing.

'If you agree to come with me it will be in a personal capacity. Not professional. But of course I will not stop your pay. When we leave Brazil you can decide how you want to proceed. You can continue to work for me or you can move on. I will give you excellent references. You will have no problem finding other work, if that's what you wish.'

Carrie felt prickly at the way he seemed to have it all worked out. 'You wouldn't have a problem with me resuming my role in a professional capacity after our affair?' Nor, apparently, with letting her go.

'Not unless you did.'

One of his lovers, upon being told that Massimo had already left the country by the time she'd woken, had said, *'Wow, he really is as cold as they say...'*

Carrie needed to remember that. She was dealing with a consummate player—even if he didn't end up splashed across the tabloids. This knowledge would protect her.

She wanted Massimo. For as long as he wanted her. What he'd given her last night—shown her about herself—was too seductive for her not to want to experience again. She knew she was weak, but this time her weakness felt like a strength. This would be for *her.*

'If I did agree, I wouldn't want you to keep paying me for the duration. It would feel...wrong. If I come with you it will be of my own accord and it will have nothing to do with our professional relationship. As for what happens afterwards... I'll see how I feel.'

In the past, she hadn't had a voice. She'd let it be silenced under layers of grief, confusion, insecurity and fear. She wouldn't let that happen again.

Massimo inclined his head, 'As you wish—and of course it'll be your decision as to what happens, Carrie.'

She felt heady, going toe to toe with Massimo and holding her own. She felt strong for the first time in a long time. She'd known that she was stronger, but she hadn't really *felt* it like this before now.

Buoyed up by that surge of power and confidence, Carrie spoke before she had time to change her mind. 'Okay, then, I'll come with you.'

Massimo found himself mesmerised by Carrie's reaction to Rio de Janeiro.

They were driving along the famous seafront and the tang of sea salt and sensuality was in the air. Carrie turned to look at him. She was wearing knee-length shorts and a sleeveless white shirt under a jacket. Mint-green. Clothes of a lover. Not her uniform. Because she was no longer his employee.

Massimo waited for a feeling of regret to hit him, but it didn't.

Her hair was down, long and tousled over her shoulders, and she went pink in the cheeks when she registered him studying her.

'You must think I'm very gauche.'

Massimo shook his head, surprised at the strength of his reaction on hearing her putting herself down. 'Not at all. This city should take everyone's breath away each time they see it.'

'But not yours.'

Her mouth quirked and Massimo had to fight the urge to haul her over onto his lap. He took his eyes off her mouth and shook his head, a familiar feeling of pain gripping his chest.

'The last time I was here my brother was here too. He was…a distraction. He had a tendency to cause a little chaos wherever he went, so I spent most of my time cleaning up his messes.'

'He died very young.'

'Ricardo died *too* young,' Massimo said grimly.

When he'd gone to identify his brother's body at the morgue in Monte Carlo, after the crash, there hadn't been one blemish or mark on his beautiful face. He'd looked as if he was sleeping. Such a waste. Such a toxic legacy. Such a failure on his behalf to save his brother.

'How old were you?'

Massimo swallowed the ball in his chest. 'Twenty-two.'

'You were young too.'

'Old enough to know that my brother had a death wish.'

'It must have been hard to watch him self-destruct.'

Massimo's chest felt tight. 'The hardest. The worst thing is knowing I could have done more to stop it.'

Carrie shook her head. 'I doubt that. If someone is hellbent on destroying themselves then they're the only ones who can stop it. When they want to. No power on earth can stop them.'

'You sound like you talk from experience.'

Carrie shook her head again. 'Not personally. I just grew up in an area where I saw it all around me. Luckily my mother kept me away from malign influences as much as possible. I saw people self-destruct, but I also saw amazing examples of people pulling themselves free—and, believe me, they had a lot less to live for than your brother did. So it can be done…but it needs to come from the person themselves.'

'Your mother was strong?'

Carrie nodded. 'The strongest.'

'Your father…?'

She tensed visibly. 'He left her as soon as he knew she was pregnant. She found out that he was married with a family. She hadn't known. She'd hoped that…'

Carrie stopped talking. Massimo could fill in the blanks. Betrayal and dashed dreams. He was surprised at the anger he felt towards the man for leaving them both like that.

After a moment, Carrie observed, 'You never went down the same self-destructive road as your brother?'

'No. I knew I had to be responsible because no one else was. I had a legacy to protect for both of us—even if he seemed intent on destroying it.'

'You made a choice, Massimo. You could have easily decided the easier path was to lose yourself.'

He'd never thought about it like that before. And suddenly he realised that they had veered into very personal territory.

Normally Massimo shut down any attempt to talk about his family—especially his brother. But she hadn't asked. He'd brought it up. He realised he trusted her. A revelation that he chose to push aside for now.

The car pulled to a stop outside a building and he said, 'We're here.'

Massimo led Carrie up to his apartment—a penthouse with panoramic views of Ipanema Beach in front and Christ the Redeemer on Mount Corcovado behind them.

'Wow…'

Carrie's eyes were wide as she took in the sleek modern furnishings and the bright pop art on the walls. She let go of his hand and walked around. Massimo opened the sliding doors that led out to a terrace, where there was a seating area and a pool.

'Wow…' she breathed again, looking out at the view.

Massimo took her hand, saying, 'And if you come up here…'

He led her up to the very top, where there was a bar area. Ric's favourite place to party. But he knew she wouldn't be interested in that.

He pointed into the distance. 'Christ The Redeemer.'

'Oh, wow…' And then, as if she'd just realised what she'd said, 'Sorry, I sound so stupid… But this is just…'

'Wow. Yes, I know.'

She scrunched up her nose a little. 'Don't take this the wrong way, but I wouldn't have had you down as owning an apartment like this.'

'That's because it wasn't always mine. It was Ric's.'

'Ah…'

'Makes more sense now?' he said dryly.

'A little.'

Massimo said, 'He loved it here. It appealed to his party side.'

'Is that why you didn't sell it?'

'I was going to, and then I realised that this place reminded me of the best of him. The joyous, excited boy he was. Before the drugs and excess took over.'

In spite of his grief, this place made Massimo feel less jaded. His brother had loved it here. Maybe that was one of the reasons. And he felt close to his memory here. Strangely, for the first time in a long time, thoughts of Ricardo weren't weighing on him as heavily. He felt lighter.

Maybe it was this woman? Maybe it was the mind-blowing sex that only seemed to be getting better? He knew that should be freaking him out on some level, but here, now, with the breeze blowing through Carrie's hair beside him and her wonderment at their surroundings, and the lingering pleasure from last night that he could still feel in his blood and bones, he couldn't seem to drum up much concern.

He pulled Carrie into him so he could feel her very feminine curves. All woman… He pushed her jacket off her shoulders and started opening her shirt. She was already a little breathless.

She said, 'When does the conference start?'

'Not for a few days,' he said, as the lace of her bra was revealed under the open shirt.

He reached inside to cup her breast, relishing the weight in his palm. It fit perfectly, the tip already a hard nub. He rubbed his thumb back and forth and Carrie's eyes started to lose focus.

'What else do you have lined up?' she asked, sounding as if she was desperately trying to cling on to some semblance of sanity. Like him.

'A hectic schedule of rest and relaxation. Wall-to-wall pleasure.'

She looked at him, her eyes focused again. 'That sounds…very lazy.'

Massimo smiled and cupped Carrie's face, lifting it towards his. Just before he covered her mouth with his, he said, 'Very, *very* lazy.'

Carrie wasn't sure if she was still human. In an embarrassingly short space of time she'd become a sloth-like sybarite. Addicted to pleasure and to the relaxed, sensual pace of Rio de Janeiro.

Everything was easy and just flowed. Minutes and hours were melting into days that had melted into…a week? More? Carrie had stopped counting.

The day after their arrival a stylist had come to the apartment with her assistants and racks of clothes for her to wear in Rio—even though a stylist had already appeared in New York to help her with a travel outfit and a suitcase of clothes to bring with her.

It appeared the Rio stylist had been instructed to provide clothes of a far more frivolous variety—swimwear that left absolutely nothing to the imagination. Underwear so light it was like air. Sparkly long dresses. Floaty kaftans.

Massimo had been at his conference for the past few days, so Carrie had got used to sleeping late, then going

Get Free Books In Just 3 Easy Steps

Are you an avid reader searching for more books?
The **Harlequin Reader Service** might be for you! We'd love to send you up to **4 free books** just for trying it out. Just write **"YES"** on the **Free Books Voucher Card** and we'll send your free books and a gift, altogether worth over $20.

Step 1: Choose your Books

Try *Harlequin® Desire* and get 2 books featuring the worlds of the American elite with juicy plot twists, delicious sensuality and intriguing scandal.

Try *Harlequin Presents® Larger-Print* and get 2 books featuring the glamorous lives of royals and billionaires in a world of exotic locations, where passion knows no bounds.

Or *TRY BOTH!*

Step 2: Return your completed Free Books Voucher Card

Step 3: Receive your books and continue reading!

Your free books are **completely free**, even the shipping! If you continue with your subscription, you can look forward to curated monthly shipments of brand-new books from your selected series, always at a discount off the cover price! Plus you can cancel any time.

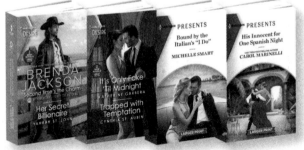

Don't miss out, reply today! Over $20 FREE value.

Free Books Voucher Card

YES! I love reading, please send me more books from the series I'd like to explore and a free gift from each series I select.

More books are just 3 steps away!

Just write in "**YES**" on the dotted line below then select your series and return this Books Voucher today and we'll send your free books & a gift asap!

YES

Choose your books:

| | Harlequin Desire® 225/326 CTI GRT3 | | Harlequin Presents® Larger-Print 176/376 CTI GRT3 | | BOTH 225/326 & 176/376 CTI G295 |

FIRST NAME

LAST NAME

ADDRESS

APT.#

CITY

STATE/PROV.

ZIP/POSTAL CODE

EMAIL ☐ Please check this box if you would like to receive newsletters and promotional emails from Harlequin Enterprises ULC and its affiliates. You can unsubscribe anytime.

HD/HP-1123-OM_123ST

across the road for a dip in the crashing surf before getting coffee and breakfast at one of the local cafés.

She loved the vibrancy of the culture here, and the way everyone smiled, and the unashamed ease they had with their bodies, no matter what size. She loved the lyrical language, and was even trying to teach it to herself via an app on her phone.

Her skin was turning golden without her even sunbathing, and a smattering of freckles she hadn't seen since she was a child were spreading across her nose.

Before Massimo had become busy with his conference he'd taken her sightseeing, up to the Redeemer statue, and he'd organised an overnight trip to see the breathtaking Iguazu Falls. Carrie still couldn't get over the natural phenomenon of the spectacular waterfalls that straddled the border between Argentina and Brazil.

But his conference was finishing today, and he was taking her out to dinner later that evening. She stretched luxuriously on the bed, entirely naked, feeling so decadent that a little giggle escaped her mouth. The huge glass doors were open to the terrace outside and a warm breeze wafted over her skin.

'Don't move.'

The voice came from the doorway. Carrie might have freaked out, but it was too familiar. She lifted her head to see Massimo, already shedding his clothes.

The fact that she didn't try to pull the sheet up over her body was testimony to how this man had rewired her brain into accepting that she was a sexual creature.

'What about the conference?'

'Last day. I bailed early.'

Gloriously naked, he strolled to the bed. Feeling utterly bold, and yet still shy, Carrie said half-heartedly, 'I haven't showered yet.'

Massimo moved over her on his hands and arms, muscles rippling. The sounds of the sea and joyous laughter drifted all the way up from outside. It infused Carrie with a sense of lightness. And then, totally unexpectedly, emotion gripped her. She realised she was grateful to Massimo for giving her this amazing experience. For restoring her womanhood back to her.

She felt free of something heavy that had weighed her down for a long time. Grief and regret. Chiefly regret. Because the grief would always be there, like a bruise that hurt sometimes more than others. But the regret she was willing to let go of. Regret for having made a bad choice in her husband…for having trusted him.

Massimo went still. He obviously saw something in her eyes. 'Hey, what is it?'

That undid her even more—that he'd noticed her emotion and stopped.

She shook her head, terrified he'd make her say it out loud. 'It's nothing… I just…'

She reached up and pulled his face down to hers and kissed him before she could make a complete fool of herself.

Thankfully, after a moment, Massimo curled one arm under her body and arched her into him as he seated himself between her legs. Then he thrust so deeply into her body that all talking and thinking became irrelevant for another few hours.

* * *

Later that evening, they had eaten dinner and were walking hand in hand through a vibrant nightlife area. An infectious samba beat spilled from countless different clubs and bars.

Carrie spotted something in a boutique window and stopped dead.

Massimo looked back. 'What is it?'

But Carrie couldn't look away. It was a dress. But not just any dress. It was the kind of dress that laid bare all the fantasies she'd kept in the deepest recesses of her imagination but would never have admitted to a living soul. It was a dress that screamed youth and fun and frivolity—things that she'd never really experienced. And it was only seeing it now, in a window in Rio de Janeiro, that made her acknowledge she'd ever even harboured such dreams.

It was pink and very short, with a deep V-neck. Pink sequins covered the material to the waist, and then pink ostrich feathers adorned the skirt which ended high on the thigh. An ostrich feather adorned its one strap.

It was ridiculous. It was audacious. And Carrie had never seen anything more beautiful.

Massimo saw what she was looking at. He said, 'It would look good on you.'

Carrie came out of her embarrassing trance. She looked away. 'No, it's ridiculous. Far too short and flashy for me.'

But Massimo was already tugging her towards the shop.

She tried to dig her heels in but it was no use. They

were in the shop, and a perky attendant was coming over. Before she knew what was happening Carrie was in a dressing room, being helped out of her own clothes and into the dress. She couldn't wear a bra. Her breasts looked positively provocative, exposed by the deep vee.

'*Muito bonita!*'

Carrie blushed in the mirror. 'I'm sorry, I don't understand.'

'You look very good.' The attendant smiled. 'You should buy.'

'Oh, I don't know—'

'We'll take it.' Massimo spoke from just outside the dressing room. And then, 'Keep it on and try these to go with it.'

A pair of shoes appeared through the curtain, perfectly matching the dress. High and sparkly. Pink. Carrie put them on and wobbled a bit, but then steadied herself.

The attendant picked up the clothes she'd been wearing—jeans and a silk top—and took them away before she could protest.

Carrie suddenly felt too shy to show herself to Massimo in the dress. As if it would just remind him of how unsophisticated she really was. She doubted any of his previous lovers would be seen dead in a dress so frilly, sparkly and short.

But then, in a fit of rebelliousness, she pulled the curtain aside and stepped out.

Massimo's eyes widened. Carrie held her breath.

But he didn't look horrified or disgusted. He looked...ravenous. Almost feral. Eyes dark and burning.

Her legs felt wobbly again.

She said, 'I can't wear this out of the shop…it's crazy.'

He shook his head and stalked towards her, putting his hands on her waist. 'We're going to go to the only place we *can* go with you in this dress.'

Carrie felt breathless. 'Where is that?'

'To a club. Not usually my style, but my brother was always moaning at me that I was too boring. I think it's time to live a little, don't you?'

Less than an hour later, Carrie and Massimo were in the most exclusive nightclub in Rio de Janeiro. A vast, high-ceilinged space with VIP booths on the first level with views of the dance floor, which was lit up with disco balls and coloured squares. It was retro, and yet effortlessly modern. Very cool.

A slick DJ was playing the glamorous crowd like a violin, choosing a series of well-known pop classics interspersed with samba beats. It was infectious. She and Massimo hadn't even drunk any alcohol, but she felt as if she'd had a bottle of champagne. Fizzing and bubbly.

He took her hand. 'Come on.'

'Where?'

He nodded towards the dance floor. 'Down there.'

Amongst the mass of heaving bodies, all moving far more sinuously than she knew how to, Carrie held back. 'I don't know, Massimo… I don't mind watching.'

But he pretended he couldn't hear her and tugged her along in his wake, all the way down the stairs and into the mass of people who moved aside to let them through.

Massimo pulled her close, hands on her hips. She gave up protesting and put her arms around his neck, bringing their bodies flush. She could feel the hard press of his arousal against her belly and moved against him, mimicking the movements of the people around them. She knew she probably looked like a total amateur, but she didn't care.

Massimo caught some of her hair and tugged her head back, so she had to look at him. He still had that slightly feral expression on his face. It sent spirals of heat and desire through her whole body. When he bent his head to kiss her, the entire nightclub fell away. It was just them…getting lost in a vortex of climbing tension and beckoning pleasure.

Massimo broke the kiss. She could feel his chest moving with his breath. Her heart was pounding.

He said, 'I think we're done with the nightclub experiment.'

Carrie couldn't argue. She let Massimo lead her back through the crowd and out of the club onto the street. She felt young and free and buoyant.

Desired.

When Massimo had hailed a cab and they were both sitting in the back, Carrie turned to him impulsively and said, 'Thank you.'

'For what?'

She felt silly now. Exposed.

She shrugged minutely. 'I never got to experience anything like this before…'

She'd never got to revel in her youth, make mistakes and live without consequence.

He frowned. 'Do you want to go back to the club?'

She shook her head and closed the space between them. 'No, I saw enough.'

He put a hand around her waist and pulled her even closer. 'Good. Because if we'd stayed there, right now we'd be giving the entire crowd a very explicit floor-show.'

He kissed her deeply, passionately, and Carrie gave herself over to the oblivion that Massimo promised and delivered over and over again.

CHAPTER SIX

'OKAY, CAN I ask where we're going now?' Carrie said.

A couple of days later she was in the back of a chauf-feur-driven car with Massimo. He'd told her to pack an overnight bag a short while before, but had been mysterious about why.

He was sitting on the other side of the car in faded jeans and a polo shirt. He looked more bronzed than usual. He looked younger. He looked ridiculously sexy.

'Yes, you can. We're going to Buenos Aires for the night—to the gala opening night of a tango show.'

Carrie's mouth opened. 'All the way to Argentina?'

'It's a three-hour flight—not too onerous. We'll have dinner and see the show.'

She was stunned. 'But I didn't bring anything with me except casual clothes.'

Massimo half smirked, half smiled. 'Don't worry, I've arranged all that.'

Carrie almost rolled her eyes. She was suddenly ter-rified of getting used to being spoiled like this. 'This is too much, Mass. You don't have to take me to Buenos Aires.' Even though she would *love* to see a tango show in the home of Argentine tango.

He reached for her. 'I like that.'

She went willingly. 'You like what?'

'What you just called me… *Mass*. My brother was the only one who used to shorten my name—except he would usually say something like, *"Mass, you're so boring..."* Or, *"Mass, you're a stick-in-the-mud."'*

Carrie's heart clenched. She could hear both love and pain in his voice. 'I wish I could have met him. I think he sounds like an amazing guy.'

'He was—and he would have liked you because you bring out a side of me that he would have approved of.'

Carrie pulled back. 'Are you saying I'm a bad influence?'

Massimo reached for her again and pulled her hand to his lap, where she could feel his body hardening against the material of his jeans.

He growled, 'You're a very bad influence.'

Carrie's mind blanked when Massimo kissed her and she welcomed it. The moment was too full of something delicate and hopeful, and she knew if she wasn't careful she would lose herself in it. Massimo was just flirting and being charming. That was *all*.

Buenos Aires was breathtaking. Carrie loved the wide streets and elegant buildings. It had a much more European feel to it than Rio de Janeiro. It felt sophisticated.

'They call it the Paris of Latin America,' Massimo said as they walked into the most opulent hotel Carrie had ever seen—apparently it had once been a palace.

One very dramatic woman, with golden skin and long, flowing brown hair, was crossing the foyer wearing a royal blue strapless silk jumpsuit with eye-wateringly high heels, and leading a dachshund by a jewelled collar.

Carrie's eyes were almost falling out of her head.

She glanced at Carrie disdainfully. Carrie couldn't blame her. She was wearing a green silk shirtdress that had felt perfectly smart in Rio, but here it felt like beach attire. And her hair was down and she wore no make-up. She felt practically feral, compared to the clientele who all oozed effortless glamour and sophistication.

A manager rushed over to greet them, and Massimo conversed with him easily in fluent Spanish. They were led up to a corner suite at the very top of the hotel, with terraces that had views over the vast city.

She wandered out to one of the terraces while Massimo issued instructions to someone on his cell phone. A profusion of plants and flowers infused the air with glorious scents, and little iridescent birds darted from flower to flower.

When the manager had left, a personal butler appeared, to enquire if they wanted anything. Carrie heard Massimo tell him that a stylist would be arriving shortly and that they'd have a late lunch on the terrace.

When they were alone again, Carrie said, 'You really don't have to spend all this money on me.'

Massimo walked over and put his hands either side of her on the wall, caging her in deliciously.

'I want to.'

Carrie grimaced. 'Let's face it…you need to, to make me look presentable.'

Massimo shook his head. 'Insecurity doesn't suit you, Carrie.'

She went still. It was such a profound thing to say to her after she'd been made to feel so insecure by someone else.

She said, 'You don't have to say that, but thank you.'

Massimo cocked his head to the side. 'Who made you feel so insecure?'

Carrie cursed her expressive features. She hadn't built up a poker face like Massimo.

He said, 'It can't have been your mother. She loved you.'

Carrie felt claustrophobic. She ducked out from under Massimo's arm and moved away. She didn't want to go there—back to the past. Not when she was enjoying the present so much. But then she thought of how generous Massimo had been, and what he'd shared about his brother.

She looked out over the city, at the people moving far below. 'My husband… It wasn't a happy marriage. At first I thought it would be—obviously, or I wouldn't have married him. But it didn't take long for him to show the real reason he'd married me.'

Because she'd been weak. Vulnerable.

'Did he hurt you?'

Massimo's voice was harsh. Carrie glanced at him. His face was stark. It sent something dangerously warm to her heart.

'No—*no*. Well, not physically, at least.' *Except for the sex you never enjoyed*, reminded a little voice.

Carrie said, 'It was mainly verbal and moods and manipulation...'

That nearly made it more humiliating. She didn't even have a physical scar to show for it.

She faced Massimo. 'Do we have to talk about this now?'

He shook his head and came towards her. 'I'm sorry you experienced that, Carrie. You didn't deserve it.'

She felt sad. 'No one ever does, do they?'

She desperately wanted Massimo to touch her, to negate the cold chill blowing over her soul, but there was a knock on the door. Massimo didn't move for a long moment and then, as if sensing what she needed—*him*—he said, 'I can send them away?'

But Carrie felt as if she was falling...slipping and sliding down a steep hill. The fact that she needed Massimo in such a very visceral way terrified her.

She pasted a bright smile on her face. 'No, don't be daft. I'm starving.'

Massimo went to answer the door and Carrie turned to face the view blindly. She wasn't falling in love. *She wasn't*. But she was in serious danger of needing Massimo in a way that had too many echoes of the past. She had to be careful...

That evening Carrie felt like a princess. After lunch a team had arrived to get her ready for the gala event that evening. And now she was wearing a long flowing chiffon evening gown. In a very light blush shade, it was whimsical and romantic, the material gathered at her waist and over her breasts by a delicate rope. Her arms were bare. Her hair was pulled back into a loose chignon. She'd been given gold drop earrings and a gold armlet.

She saw herself in the mirror and felt a jolt. It was so strange to see herself transformed like this. It felt right…but it also felt wrong. More wrong than right.

Massimo walked into the room, resplendent in a black tuxedo, fixing his cuffs. He saw her and stopped in his tracks, dark eyes moving over her so thoroughly that it felt like a caress. But not even that could shake the uncomfortable sensation that she didn't really belong here.

His gaze narrowed. 'What is it? You look as if you've seen a ghost.'

She gestured to herself. 'This isn't me. I feel like I'm in the wrong place and it's only a matter of time before I'm asked to leave.'

He moved towards her. 'You know what they call that?'

She shook her head.

'Imposter syndrome.'

'Well, that's because I am an imposter.'

He shook his head. 'You have as much right as anyone else to be in this place.'

'I don't belong here.'

'And I do belong here just because of an accident of birth? That's not very fair, is it?'

Carrie shook her head.

Massimo reached out and cupped her neck, tugging

her gently towards him. The dress whispered around her body, in a sensual reminder of the woman this man had awoken.

'You're here because I asked you and you said yes. You want to be here, don't you?'

She knew that she did. In spite of all her doubts and feeling that she didn't belong. Carrie nodded slowly. She did want to be here, and she'd chosen to be here.

'Good,' Massimo said, and he lowered his mouth to hers before whispering against her lips, 'Because you are beautiful, and there's no one else I'd want to be here with me right now.'

Carrie's chest swelled with an unnamed emotion, but she pulled away from his kiss even though it killed her. 'Please don't say things like that, Mass. I don't need to hear it.'

I want to hear it...too much.

Massimo looked at her for a long moment, his face unreadable. Eventually he said, 'Fine.'

They left the suite and Massimo only lightly touched her on her back as they walked out of the hotel to the car.

She felt as if she'd broken something, but it was better this way.

Sitting in a box seat at the theatre in Buenos Aires a short while later, Massimo was still feeling exposed. No woman had ever complained before when he'd issued a compliment. Although he'd spent so little time with any of them that it wasn't usually necessary.

But what he'd said to Carrie earlier, he'd meant. He

really didn't want to be here with anyone else. And it had spilled from his mouth as easily as breathing. *She'd* been the one to pull back. Say there was no need.

What the hell was wrong with him? Did he want her to fall for him? *No way.* And yet the way he was behaving anyone would be forgiven for thinking he was waging an all-out campaign. He'd never seduced a woman so comprehensively.

He looked at the stage. The hauntingly beautiful strains of the music of Astor Piazzolla, one of the world's most famous tango composers, mocked him now. Mocked him for being complacent. For losing his mind for a moment.

The couple onstage danced, their bodies moving in sync, twining erotically before coming apart again, then melding again so closely that it was hard to see where one ended and the other began.

Massimo glanced at Carrie and his gaze narrowed. There was moisture in her eyes. The melancholic music would affect the stoniest of hearts. Ricardo, his brother, had found it deadly boring but Massimo had always found it moving.

His brother had teased him once. 'Admit it, Mass, you're a secret romantic!'

Massimo had put Ricardo in a head-lock.

But it looked as if Carrie, for all her protests at being complimented, was a secret romantic too. Or maybe she was still lamenting her toxic relationship with her husband.

Massimo hadn't expected her to reveal that he'd been abusive. The white-hot surge of anger he'd felt when he'd believed he might have hurt her had surprised him. Still surprised him.

All through his parents' volatile marriage they hadn't ever been physically violent with each other. Which was about the only saving grace of that marriage.

But the fact that it had been mental abuse rather than physical in Carrie's case didn't make it any better, of course. Mental scars left deeper wounds.

If anything, she'd done him a favour—reminding him of what this was. An affair. A deeper one than he would have expected, granted. But just an affair.

The couple on the stage moved into a classic Argentine tango pose as the last strains of the music faded away. Carrie felt hollowed out and wrung dry. She'd never expected a dance and its music to affect her so deeply.

She'd found herself desperately trying to suppress her emotions and, worse, her tears. But it had been almost impossible. The exquisitely beautiful dance, together with the most melancholic music, had touched every deep and hidden yearning she'd ever had. Regret, her loss and grief. And, the pain of confusing the need for security with love which had ended in tragedy.

She avoided looking at Massimo when he reached for her hand to lead her out.

Their car was waiting for them, and as it moved smoothly into the Buenos Aires traffic Carrie felt a little more composed.

From the other side of the car, Massimo said, 'You were moved by the performance?'

Carrie cursed him for noticing. He noticed too much.

She glanced at him. He was watching her. She'd noticed him watching her a few times during the evening and wondered if perhaps he was insulted that she'd rebuffed his compliment earlier.

She turned to face him. 'Look, about earlier, I didn't mean to sound—'

But Massimo cut her off. 'I think it's the music. It has that effect on people. You know the dance originated among the migrants and slaves in the poor areas of the city? Men danced it together because there were no women. Its roots are European and African. I'm not remotely romantic, but that music more than any other has the power to make me believe that romance exists.'

'I'm not remotely romantic.'

A clear message that he knew what she had been about to say.

So she said, 'I'm not remotely romantic either.'

She certainly wasn't. Not any more—if she ever had been. So why did that assertion cause a little pang in her chest? As if she was betraying some part of herself?

She ignored it.

She could see their hotel in the distance, and then Massimo surprised her by saying, 'We could go straight back to Rio now, if you like? Wake up there in the morning. Or we could stay here for the night?'

Carrie didn't want to leave Buenos Aires. But the truth was that this city seemed to evoke in her too many emotions and revelations for her liking.

She said, 'Would you mind if we went back to Rio?'

Massimo shook his head. 'Not at all. I can have the

hotel pack our things and send them on. We can sleep on the plane.'

He took her hand and lifted it, pressing a kiss to the palm. It felt shockingly intimate.

And then he said, 'Or not sleep…it's your choice.'

The car turned around to head in the other direction and Carrie felt inordinately relieved—as if she was escaping her conscience and her emotions.

Coward, whispered a voice.

She ignored it. 'I'm not that tired, actually.'

Massimo put his hands on her waist and pulled her close. 'That's funny, I'm not either…'

As soon as the plane hit a certain altitude Massimo undid his belt buckle and stood up, holding out a hand to Carrie. He'd taken off his jacket and bow-tie. His shirt was undone. Stubble lined his jaw. He looked uncharacteristically roguish.

She put her hand in his and let him pull her up. She should have felt ridiculous on a plane in full evening dress, but she didn't. It seemed that nothing fazed her any more. It was as if something had just happened between them. A clarification.

This is just an affair. We're not romantics. We know what's happening. We're in control.

Massimo led her into the bedroom suite, where there was a massive walk-in shower. He let her hand go and went and turned it on. Steam quickly filled the space.

Carrie realised the audacity of what they were about to do. 'The cabin crew won't disturb us?'

'They know not to.'

Ouch.

An even clearer reminder that she wasn't the first woman Massimo had done this with and wouldn't be the last.

In a bid to hide how that made her feel, she started to take down her hair. Massimo watched her as her hair fell down around her shoulders. She shook it out. Then she found the zip at the side of her dress and pulled it down. The dress fell to her feet in a soft swish of expensive fabric.

She stepped out of the shoes. Now all she wore was a strapless bra and matching briefs. Mere wisps of material.

Feeling bold under Massimo's hungry gaze, and aware of how finite all this was, Carrie turned and walked straight into the shower.

She turned around and Massimo looked almost feral as he took in the water sluicing down over her body, turning her underwear completely translucent. She might as well have been naked.

He didn't wait. He ripped off his clothes and they scattered around him. Gloriously naked and aroused, he stepped into the shower with Carrie. Dispensing with her underwear with a mere flick of his wrist, he caught her under her arms and lifted her up.

'Lean back against the wall.'

She did. Her legs were shaking now. She wrapped them around his waist. Water flattened his hair to his head. His cheeks were slashed with colour.

For her.

He bent his head and took the hard tip of one breast

into his mouth, rolling and sucking the peak until Carrie's mind was blissfully blank of anything but this devastating pleasure.

Her hips were moving against Massimo, seeking for him to assuage the spiralling tension at her core. He put his hand there, against her body, feeling how ready she was for him. Sliding his fingers deep, making her moan.

And then he took himself in his hand and fed himself into her, inch by inch, until she couldn't breathe. She was impaled, and it was delicious.

Slowly he moved in and out, bearing her weight with an arm around her waist. It didn't take long. She could feel the swell approaching, gathering force, and she had to bite down on his shoulder to stop herself from screaming out loud as the waves pounded over her and through her.

Massimo's body moved against her powerfully as he sought his own climax, and then he pulled free abruptly, making Carrie gasp, and let the powerful jet spray wash away his climax.

It hadn't even occurred to her to think of protection—the feel of his body within hers had been too exquisite. And now she was too spent to dwell on it. She would have slid down the wall of the shower if Massimo hadn't caught her and lifted her into his arms.

He sat her down and took a towel, drying her and then scooping her hair up into another towel. He carried her from the bathroom to the bed and placed her down, and for a fleeting moment before Carrie lost consciousness she thought to herself that it was the kindest thing she could remember anyone doing for her for a long time...

* * *

'I need to go back to New York for some meetings.'

Carrie's insides sank.

She'd known this was coming. They'd been back in Rio for over a week now. She'd been wondering how long Massimo could duck out of his life.

She'd worked it out that morning: they'd actually been away for a month. She'd been on holiday for one month. More time off than she'd ever had in her life. But they couldn't exist in this sensual tropical idyll for ever.

She affected a look of polite uninterest, as if his pronouncement wasn't sounding the death knell on their relationship. 'Okay…when?'

'Today, actually.'

Her insides lurched even more. Not even another day or night?

The sound of the crashing surf from Ipanema mocked her from the background.

'You'll come with me,' Massimo pronounced.

Carrie felt prickly. 'Will I? It's about time I thought about what I'm going to do next.'

'This doesn't have to end yet. Come back to New York with me. You'll have plenty of time to think about the future.'

Her treacherous heart squeezed.

Maybe it wouldn't be over yet, but it would be soon.

She could feel it like the inevitability of a rising tide. And she was in way too deep. Any control she might have exerted over this whole situation was well and truly gone.

Buenos Aires and then these last few days in Rio with Massimo had dismantled all her very careful defences, leaving her nowhere to hide. And, as much as she knew it would be wiser to take the initiative here and be the one to leave first, she knew she wasn't ready to walk away from Massimo and the way he made her feel.

He'd opened up her eyes to a whole world of experience—and not just sexually. She'd changed. Relaxed. Found a measure of peace she'd never expected. Selfishly, she wasn't ready to let that go, because she knew that whatever happened to her after this, and wherever she went, she would never experience that again.

Still trying to affect a cool level of nonchalance, even though she knew what she was about to do spelled certain pain and humiliation in the future, she said, 'Okay, why not?'

'Good.'

Massimo's satisfied, knowing smile, as if he'd known exactly what she'd been thinking, made her want to wipe it off his face. So she did.

She got up from her chair and let her robe fall open enough so that he could see her bare breasts. She sat on his lap and said throatily, 'Exactly how long do we have before we leave?'

Massimo's eyes were burning and his arms were snaking around her waist, holding her tight. 'Long enough.'

He picked her up into his arms and took her back to the bedroom, and Carrie exulted in this very minor measure of control she wielded.

* * *

Even though it had only been a few weeks since they'd been in New York, the seasons were changing. The humid heat was gone and the air was much milder. Fresher. Carrie felt as if she'd been abroad for ever. Her old life and her work as Massimo's housekeeper felt very far away.

This was reinforced when they went into the apartment and the new male housekeeper met them, treating Carrie with deference, as if she was Massimo's mistress.

Which you are, pointed out a snarky voice.

'Miss Taylor, if you'll give me your dietary preferences, I'll pass them on to Chef.'

Carrie blushed when she thought of what Chef would make of her new status. She said quickly, 'That's really not necessary. I eat everything and anything.'

'No allergies?'

'No.'

He looked almost comically disappointed. Carrie might have laughed if she hadn't been feeling a little nauseous after the journey. She'd asked exactly the same questions of Massimo's guests, countless times.

When the housekeeper had left, Massimo said, 'I have to go straight to the office now, but we can eat out later if you like.'

To Carrie's surprise, she felt a surge of queasiness at the thought of eating out. She shook her head, 'That's really not necessary. I'm happy to eat in.'

She realised she was feeling quite tired too, all of a sudden. A very faint warning bell went off in her head, but she couldn't put a finger on what it meant.

'I'm happy just to potter here.'

Massimo frowned. 'Potter? You are making pottery?'

Carrie laughed. 'No, silly. *Potter*—as in mooch about, doing things with no real aim.' She saw the confusion on his face and took pity. 'Don't worry about it. The concept doesn't really exist in your world.'

He grinned, and the sight of it took Carrie's breath away for a moment.

He tugged her close. 'That's a pity…maybe you can teach me more about this *pottering* later. Does it apply to bed?'

Carrie giggled. 'Not really.'

She realised they were both grinning at each other. A swell of emotion gripped her before she could stop it.

She took a step back, rearranged her face. 'You should probably get going…'

To her surprise, Massimo reached out and traced a finger down over her cheek to her jaw, leaving her skin tingling.

'Later, then.'

She felt breathless, and wondered how he could still have this effect on her when she now knew his body as intimately as her own. 'Okay, then, later…'

His hand dropped and he walked out.

Carrie lifted her hand to her face and touched where he'd touched. It had been a tender gesture. Not even sexual. Like when her mother had used to tuck hair behind her ear. It made her feel—dangerously—a kernel of hope.

But for what? asked a questioning voice.

She sat down on a chair, suddenly deflated.

Massimo had made it very clear he didn't want a relationship, and even though she might want to try again at some stage, he was way out of her league. He didn't have relationships. He had lovers. Yet, no matter what he'd told Carrie, he would marry a woman from among his peers eventually. At some point he would realise that he had a responsibility to carry on the Linden title.

Massimo might be happy to keep her on as his mistress indefinitely, while he wanted her, but it would come to an end. And Carrie knew now that she would have to be the one to take the initiative. To walk away. Because if Massimo kept touching her like that she would be right back at square one. Believing in things that didn't exist.

But maybe not today, she told herself weakly. Surely another few days couldn't hurt?

Telling herself that maybe a nap would help ease the queasiness, she went up to the room she'd used before. She dithered on the threshold when she couldn't see any of her bags or other things.

Curious, she went up to Massimo's room—and there they were. Already laid out by the unseen hands that did this kind of thing in his world. The unseen hands that had used to be hers.

All the beautiful clothes she'd been given were hanging up in his dressing room…laid out in drawers. Her toiletries were lined up in his bathroom beside the other sink.

Overcome with another wave of fatigue, Carrie put it down to the whirlwind of the last few weeks and took off her clothes to slip into a robe. She washed her face and climbed into one side of Massimo's massive bed. She was asleep before her head hit the pillow.

When Massimo returned to the apartment later that evening it was quiet. Very quiet. He moved through the downstairs rooms and they were empty. The chef had left, having been instructed that they would be fending for themselves.

The new housekeeper had also left.

The apartment was exactly as it had always been after he'd been away on trips before.

He'd never invited a woman into this space unless it was just for the night, but he couldn't see any traces of Carrie anywhere and that was disconcerting. She'd left more traces of herself when she'd been his housekeeper. Shoes by the front door. Flowers on the table. A throw over a chair in the kitchen.

But he realised now that she'd been tidied away by the staff—just as his things were tidied away all the time. So that wherever he went it was always pristine.

For the first time in his life he resented that. He wanted to walk into a room and see a book left open on a table. Or cushions out of place. Signs of life.

Massimo smiled a mirthless smile when he thought of his little brother, who would undoubtedly have welcomed this desire for a little messiness.

He took off his jacket and draped it over the back of a chair. Then he undid his top button, pulled off his tie and left that hanging over another chair. He had a sudden urge to find Carrie and bring her here, into the living room, so they could really mess it up by making love on every couch and chaise longue. Ricardo would approve.

But when he stuck his head into the kitchen it too was silent and empty, except for the hum of the appliances. Massimo had never really noticed that before…

A thought occurred to him. Maybe she'd gone out? To do this…*pottering*. Her independence was something that he liked about her, but an uneasy sensation moved through him as he went to her bedroom and found it untouched.

For a second he imagined that she'd changed her mind and just left…and the lurch in his gut was not welcome. It shouldn't bother him if Carrie had decided to end their relationship. It had transgressed so many boundaries that he had no right to expect her to stay.

But he wasn't ready to let her go.

Not by a long shot.

He went up to his bedroom. He hesitated at the door for a moment, before telling himself he was being ridiculous and opening it.

The first thing he saw was a shape in the bed. *Carrie*. She was here. Just asleep.

He walked over and looked down. She was on her back, one arm flung up by her head, her hair spread out around her head in a halo of gold waves. Her face was clean of make-up. He could see the spatter of freckles across her nose. The sun-kissed glow.

He ignored the sense of relief. *Not* relief. Desire.

He sat down on the side of the bed and she stirred,

eyes flickering and then opening. She saw him and it took a second for her to come wide awake.

She sat up, slightly groggy. 'I fell asleep…what time is it?'

Massimo noticed that actually, underneath the sun-kissed glow, she was a little pale. 'Are you okay?'

She frowned. 'I think so… I was just really tired all of a sudden, so I lay down.'

'Are you hungry?'

She absorbed this—and then, with almost comical speed, she went green and leapt out of the bed and into the bathroom, slamming the door behind her.

Massimo winced at the sounds that ensued. He would have gone in, but he had a feeling Carrie wouldn't appreciate it.

She emerged a few minutes later with her hair pulled back, looking very pale.

Massimo jumped up. 'You're not well. I'll call a doctor.'

She put out a hand. 'No, it's nothing serious. It's just food poisoning or a bug.'

'But I'm okay and we've eaten all the same things.'

'I'm sure it's nothing…'

She looked as if she was about to collapse.

Massimo reached out and grabbed her, leading her back to the bed and letting her lie down.

But she struggled to sit up again. 'I should go to my own room.'

Massimo pushed her back down, gently. 'No way. This is your room. What can I get you?'

Carrie said, 'Maybe just a little water and a dry biscuit, if there's anything like that?'

Massimo pulled the robe over Carrie's chest, where
it was gaping open, showing the curves of her breasts.
Not now. He went and pulled a pair of silk pyjamas
from a drawer and came back, helping her to sit on the
side of the bed.

'You'll be more comfortable in these.'

With superhuman strength, he managed to help
her out of the robe and into the pyjamas without turning into a caveman. He left her in bed and went to the
kitchen to get the water and a biscuit—which, of course,
took him an age, because he couldn't find the pantry
where the dry goods were kept.

When he got back upstairs, though, Carrie was
asleep again, so he left the water on the table, with
a couple of biscuits on a plate, and went to his study.

He'd never been in this situation before…

During the night Carrie woke and had a little water
and some of the biscuits. She said to Massimo, 'I'm sure
by the morning I'll be feeling much better…'

CHAPTER SEVEN

BUT WHEN CARRIE woke at dawn she wasn't feeling better at all. She managed to get to the bathroom just in time.

When she'd finished being sick she stood up and looked at her wan features in the mirror. She could only remember feeling this sick once before, and her whole body went cold as she realised it.

She put her hand on her belly. *No.* The universe wouldn't be so cruel, would it?

She went back out into the bedroom and saw Massimo standing there, bare-chested, wearing sleep pants that hung low on his hips. For the first time Carrie didn't feel a sizzle. She felt even queasier.

She only realised Massimo was talking into a mobile phone when he said, 'Okay, Doctor, thank you.'

Carrie went cold. 'Who was that?'

'My doctor is coming to see you.'

'But it's really nothing,' protested Carrie, while silently saying a prayer that it wasn't the potentially huge thing she feared it could be.

She climbed back into bed, feeling too weak to stand and face a brooding Massimo.

'I'm really sorry about this.'

It wasn't exactly lover/mistress behaviour.

Massimo frowned. 'Don't be silly. I'm going to take a shower and then wait for the doctor.'

Carrie lay back on the bed and tried not to let her mind go to scary places. She felt numb. Which was a bit of a relief after the constant queasiness. But if this was what she feared it was, this stage would pass soon enough…

Carrie looked at herself in the bathroom mirror again. She'd had a shower and was dressed in faded jeans and a shirt. Hair still damp and loose around her shoulders. She looked marginally better. She felt marginally better. At least physically.

Emotionally was another story.

She'd just had her fears confirmed by the doctor and the doctor's handy little pregnancy test, which had very definitively spelled out *PREGNANT* on its digital display.

The wonders of modern technology…able to diagnose a pregnancy even at this early stage…

He'd said he thought she was about a month in, so Carrie had dated conception back to when they'd first slept together in New York. The moment when Massimo had thrust inside her before remembering to put on protection.

She hadn't even realised she'd missed a period.

There was a knock on the door. 'Carrie?'

Her belly lurched—but not with nausea this time. With fear and trepidation.

She called out, 'I'm fine. I'll see you downstairs.'

Hesitation outside. Then, 'I'll have Chef prepare some tea and toast.'

Carrie put a hand to her mouth to contain a semi-hysterical giggle at the thought of how things had veered so off-course. But then she sobered again when she thought about telling Massimo. She had no choice. His doctor knew, and even though he wouldn't have told Massimo she couldn't sit on this. It was too huge.

She went downstairs and found Massimo in the private media room. He was dressed in jeans and a long-sleeved top, his hair mussed as if he'd been running a hand through it. He was watching a news channel, but switched it off when she came in. He stood up.

Carrie opened her mouth, but at that moment the chef appeared with a tray of tea and toast. He put it down on the coffee table by the couch.

Carrie smiled at him weakly, not sure what he must be thinking about this reversal of her status. He was discreet, though, as were all of Massimo's staff. As she had once been.

When he'd left, Massimo said, 'Sit down...have something.'

Carrie felt like just blurting it out there and then, but Massimo looked concerned, and she knew she needed to fortify herself for whatever reaction she was going to get. So she dutifully sat down and had some tea and buttered toast. It tasted like cardboard in her mouth.

After she'd had a few mouthfuls, Massimo said, 'So...what is it?'

Carrie wiped her mouth with a napkin. She looked at Massimo. Only about a foot separated them on the couch. He was too close.

She stood up and walked over to stand behind an armchair.

Massimo stood too. 'Carrie...?'

'It's nothing serious.' She thought about that, 'Well... that's not exactly true.'

Massimo frowned. 'Carrie, what the...?

'I'm pregnant.'

Her words hung between them. Massimo looked confused. 'What did you say?'

Carrie's hands gripped the back of the seat. 'I'm pregnant.'

Massimo shook his head. 'But...how? I used protection every time.'

Carrie thought again of that moment—the second time they'd made love.

Massimo's face darkened. 'There was only *one* instance, and I made sure to put on protection as soon as I remembered.'

But that was all it took. A moment.

Weakly, she said, 'No form of protection is one hundred per cent reliable.'

He looked at her. His face stark. 'You don't seem surprised.'

Carrie took stock of what she was feeling. Shocked? She shook her head. 'It's not something I considered even a remote possibility.'

Massimo didn't say anything for a long moment, and then, 'Are you sure about that?'

'What's that supposed to mean?'

Massimo's expression was stone. 'Did you set out to trap me?'

Carrie was flabbergasted, and hurt that his cynicism would take him to that conclusion.

She found her voice eventually. 'Why on earth would I want to trap you?'

'To be set for life? To never have to worry about anything ever again?'

Carrie came out from behind the chair, incensed. 'Why, you arrogant bastard! You think wealth can stop anything bad from happening? That wealth magically insulates you from ill-health or loss?' She pointed at him. 'You know better than most how that's not true. All wealth does is insulate you from doing your own dirty washing! Or having to use public transport. Or talking to normal people and realising that maybe not everything is about you!'

Massimo folded his arms across his chest. Her words seemed to have made no impact.

'Like I said...you don't seem surprised.'

Because on some level she wasn't. Because she'd known it even before she'd allowed herself to think it. Because it was exactly what had happened before.

Considering where they were now, she knew she would have to tell Massimo everything.

Massimo wasn't sure how he was still standing when he felt as if a million rugs had just been pulled from under his feet. The last time he'd felt this blindsided had been when they'd told him that Ric had died—and even that hadn't come as such a huge shock.

Which somehow made this level of shock feel like a betrayal.

He also felt exposed. *Again.* He'd been so careful never to let anyone too close. When he'd realised he hadn't been able to trust his own parents, he'd learnt a very early lesson in depending on himself. Ric was the only person who had breached Massimo's defences, and he'd vowed never to endure the pain of that kind of loss again.

Yet he'd been letting Carrie sneak right under those defences for weeks now.

Her words mocked him, *'You think wealth can stop anything bad from happening? That wealth magically insulates you from ill-health or loss?'*

Of course he knew it didn't. But he also knew that wealth could make those things a lot easier to bear. And right now it seemed crystal-clear to him that he'd vastly underestimated the sweet and innocent Carrie Taylor.

She was just like everyone else who'd circled like vultures as soon as his father's death had been announced. Women looking for a rich lover, or better yet a husband. Men looking for a deal. Charities looking for handouts. He'd decided to focus on charities because at least that was transparent...

'Well?' he prompted.

He could see the emotion on Carrie's face. Anger. Because he could see right through her. He pushed away the pricking of his conscience that he was letting his own anger skew his judgement.

She closed her mouth. Swallowed. Turned away.

He wanted to go over to her and demand she look him in the eye and spout her lies.

She turned around again, but still avoided his eye. She said quietly, 'I was pregnant before and the symptoms were the same.'

That took a second to sink in. And then the thought of her being pregnant with another man's child sent a series of conflicting emotions through Massimo.

'With your husband?' he asked.

She nodded. 'Four years ago.'

'You came to work for *me* four years ago.'

'Six months before I came to be interviewed for the job.'

'What happened?'

Carrie looked at him. Her eyes looked bruised.

She said, 'I was three months pregnant. My husband and I were involved in a car crash. That's how he died. And I miscarried. We were arguing. I had just told him I wanted to leave him, even though I was pregnant.'

She'd blamed herself for what had happened for a long time, but now she knew it hadn't been her fault. It had just been a tragic accident.

Massimo's anger drained away, leaving just shock. He could remember what she'd been like four years ago. Painfully thin. Pale. Delicate.

'I'm sorry he died like that...and that you lost your baby.'

She said, 'If my ambition all along had been to seduce you and trap you, I'd like to think I would have done it before now and not waited four years.'

Massimo didn't like the logic of that. He had to concede that he'd overreacted. He said, 'I'm sorry for accusing you of premeditating this. I know you better than that.'

She swallowed. 'I know it's a shock. It's a shock for me too, no matter what it might look like. I hadn't ever thought I'd be pregnant again.'

Pregnant.

The concept of such a thing was too huge for Massimo to contemplate right now.

'Why? You'd make a great mother.'

Carrie shrugged minutely. 'After…what happened, I vowed never to marry again. I won't trust anyone that much again. I almost lost myself in the process before, and as it was I lost too much.'

'Do you want to keep it?'

He heard the words come out of his mouth but couldn't recall having the thought.

She flinched and looked at him accusingly. 'Of course. I lost one baby. I won't lose another if I can help it. And it's not an *it*. She or he is a baby. Your son or daughter.'

His baby.

Massimo's head throbbed. He needed to push her away. Push this whole thing away.

He said abruptly, 'I have to go to a meeting this morning. We'll continue our conversation later.'

He walked out of the room and left the apartment.

It was only when he reached his office and he noticed people looking at him that he realised he was still wearing jeans and a light jumper. He never appeared at the office in anything less formal than a suit. He'd vowed never to give anyone the opportunity to question his dedication or his professionalism after his father had decimated the family's reputation.

He felt exposed.

When Massimo got to his floor he bit out instructions to his assistant. 'Hold all my meetings and do not disturb me.'

He went into his office and straight to the drinks cabinet. He poured himself a generous mouthful of whisky and downed it in one. Then another. As the fiery liquid burned its way down his throat and into his chest he poured another and went over and looked out of the window, not seeing anything.

His brain felt like a solid rock in his head. His chest was tight. Every muscle tense.

The very thing he'd told himself he would never, *ever* pursue—a family—was now a very unwelcome possibility. And Massimo knew he had no choice but to accept this new reality and protect his legacy.

Carrie heard Massimo's arrival back to the apartment. She was sitting in the formal reception room, waiting. She felt calm. She knew that it was most likely still shock. But she would take it. Just so she could deal with this next bit.

She stood up.

One thing was certain: whatever had been between

them, still electric and alive only yesterday, was well and truly dead now.

Massimo came into the room and saw her. He stopped. He looked more dishevelled than he had earlier. A little wild. Carrie couldn't stop a sizzle of awareness. It was back, in spite of the acute morning sickness and everything else that had happened.

Massimo looked her over and she stood tall. She was dressed in the same clothes she'd worn to come to New York. Work clothes. Smart. Hair tied back.

He said, 'Where are you going?'

Carrie looked down at her compact suitcase. And then up to him. 'I'm going back to London.'

'And what's your plan when you get there?'

Fear and not a little panic gripped Carrie. 'To find a place to live and a job.'

Massimo shook his head. 'That's not how this is going to play out.'

'It isn't?'

'No.' He looked at her, eyes narrowed. 'We are going to get married.'

Carrie might have fallen backwards if the couch hadn't been behind her legs. She saw something in his eyes—determination.

She shook her head and moved away from the couch. 'No way. That is not the solution.'

'Do I need to remind you of who I am? Once this gets out it'll make headlines.'

Carrie's level of panic rose by several notches. 'Well, it's not going to get out unless you tell anyone. There is no way I would agree to marry you, because you've made it quite clear that you never want to marry, and also, as I told you, I vowed never to marry again. I will never allow myself to be made vulnerable again—and marriage makes you vulnerable.'

'I can't dispute that,' Massimo said grudgingly.

'Good, then you agree.'

'No, I don't agree. It just means we're both on the same page. We'll know that we're only doing this for the sake of our child.'

'A marriage based on duty is no place for a child to be brought up. Children need love and security. Happy parents.'

'We survived in less than ideal circumstances.'

'I wouldn't be so sure about that,' Carrie commented.

Massimo couldn't seem to answer that. He said, 'And where would I be in this non-marriage scenario?'

'You would be part of our child's life. I would never deny you that—especially not after my own father rejected me.'

'So how will this work, exactly, with me in the child's life but not really part of it? Do we live near one another? How does access work?'

Carrie's head started to hurt. 'We can work all that out.'

'And how are you going to cope with your pregnancy? How will you survive when you become too pregnant to work?'

Carrie lifted her chin. 'I will manage. My mother coped just fine with a lot less. I won't expect anything from you until the baby is born. Anything could happen—as I know.'

'That is not a viable plan, Carrie. Marrying me would give us control of the situation in case the news leaks out, and also give you security and protection while you're pregnant.'

The thought of being wedded to this man who clearly despised her now sent bile through Carrie's guts. She already knew what it was like to be rejected by one man—her father—and then used as a thing to dominate by another man—her husband.

She lifted her chin. 'You couldn't pay me to marry you.'

Massimo's face darkened. 'Not even...?'

He named an astronomical amount of money. A life-changing amount of money.

Carrie felt sick. 'You know, up until this moment I actually believed you had integrity, but you're really not so different to your family, are you?'

Massimo's face was like stone. 'If you're saying you can't be bought, then you might as well admit to being a mythical unicorn. Everyone has a price.'

Carrie felt sad. She shook her head. 'Not me. My price is my baby being born healthy and having enough to live on and get by.'

'Without me.'

'I'm not saying that. I would want you to be part of his or her life.'

Massimo paced back and forth. He stopped and looked at Carrie. 'I might never have planned on having a family, because I don't want to pass down whatever destructive genes I might carry, but I will not shirk my responsibility.'

Carrie's heart lurched. 'You don't carry any destructive genes.'

Massimo dismissed her comment with a wave of his hand. 'I need to know that you are both safe and well. I need to be able to control the PR in case something is leaked to the press. Do you have any idea of what a child of mine stands to inherit? This isn't just about you any more, Carrie.'

She balked at that. She really hadn't got her head around the fact that her baby would be heir to a vast legacy.

She put her hand over her belly instinctively, as if to shield the child within from its own future. And a reluctant father.

And then something came to her—a compromise. She said carefully, 'It's clear now that whatever was between us is…over?'

'Yes.'

The speed with which he agreed sent a little knife into her gut, but she ignored it. It was better this way. What if he actually tried to charm her into marrying him? She wouldn't have a hope. At least he was being honest.

'I have a solution…if you're willing to agree to it.'

Six weeks later

Massimo pulled his car into the forecourt of his London home. He was tense. He'd been tense for weeks now. Tense and something else he didn't quite want to admit to. But he knew what it was: sexual frustration. A sexual frustration that only one woman could alleviate.

He got out of the car. A distinct chill in the air and the leaves on the ground foretold of winter settling in, but he noticed none of that. He approached the immaculately glossy black front door and it opened as if operated by some kind of magical device. But there was no magic—just his housekeeper, Carrie, on the threshold. She was dressed in her uniform of black shirt and black trousers. Flat shoes. Blonde hair pulled back neatly in a bun at the base of her neck. No overt make-up. No jewellery.

She had no discernible expression on her face. 'Welcome back, sir.'

The sense of déjà-vu was strong enough to almost knock him backwards. Had he in fact imagined the last couple of months? Had he imagined the best sex he'd ever had?

No. His blood was humming to see her again. The one woman he wanted and the one woman he couldn't have.

He looked at her midriff. Was it thicker? With his child?

An unsettling feeling of pride took him unawares.

He'd spent the last six weeks mired in crisis after crisis that had kept him from coming back to London.

He'd spent the last six weeks trying not to think about the fact that he was going to be a father, whether he liked it or not.

On the one hand he had to admit he'd welcomed the

distraction, but on the other hand he'd felt rudderless. And for the first time in his life *lonely*. A new concept.

But every time he'd spoken to Carrie on the phone she'd been breezy, as if there was nothing strange about the fact that they'd agreed to her continuing to work as his housekeeper. He'd only accepted her proposal because it was that or she was going to leave entirely and make her own way.

He walked into the house. Her scent caught him. The same scent. Uncomplicated. But nothing about this situation was uncomplicated. Her calmness made him feel volatile.

He said, 'Can we talk? In my office?'

'Of course,' she said smoothly. 'Shall I bring you a coffee?'

Massimo felt like snapping, *No, get someone else to bring it*, but he forced himself to be civil. 'Yes, sure, a coffee would be lovely. Thank you.'

Carrie went towards the kitchen and Massimo undid and ripped off his tie as he went to his office. He took off his jacket and paced back and forth, full of restless energy in spite of a transatlantic flight.

A light knock on the door and Carrie came in with a tray. She put it down on the table and stood back.

'Please, sit down.'

Clearly reluctant to do so, she finally did. On the edge of a seat on the other side of the table.

Massimo sat down too and took a sip of coffee. He studied Carrie, which was easy to do when she was looking anywhere but at him. She looked…well. Really well. Pink in her cheeks. Eyes bright.

His gaze moved down. Her breasts looked bigger. Did that happen in pregnancy? The thought of her body growing ripe with his child sent another unsettling wave of a mixture of pride and possession through him. But underlying it all was desire.

He still wanted her.

He'd wanted her even when she'd dropped the bombshell of her pregnancy.

'How are you?' he asked.

She looked at him, a little startled, as if she'd forgotten he was in the room. Massimo clenched his jaw. Her eyes looked greener.

'I'm... I'm okay, thanks.'

'Have you been sick again?'

She shook her head. 'No, thankfully it was just that twenty-four hours. It was the same the last time. Luckily.'

'How is it being housekeeper again?'

'It's fine. Totally fine.'

'So this...arrangement is working for you?'

Carrie knotted her hands together in her lap. It had been working a lot better when Massimo wasn't here. She'd had space to come to terms with everything that had happened and to try and convince herself that any desire she'd felt had died along with their affair.

But that had been wishful thinking. The moment she'd seen him uncoil his tall frame from the car on his arrival it was as if she'd been plugged back into an electrical mainframe. It had taken all her composure to open the door and let him in and not tremble when his scent washed over her.

Even now she wanted to let her gaze rove over every inch of him. Was his hair longer? Did he look tired? Was there stubble on his jaw?

Had he been with another woman?

That question made her feel queasy. Maybe she did still have morning sickness…

She gathered her wits to answer him. 'It's working fine. But if you're not comfortable—'

'No,' he said abruptly, cutting her off. 'It's fine for now. The scan is this afternoon, right?'

She nodded. 'After lunch.'

She didn't like that ominous-sounding, *It's fine for now.*

Massimo said, 'I'll drive us there.'

'You don't have to come if you're too busy.'

He looked at her. 'I'm coming to my baby's first scan.'

My baby.

What had happened in six weeks? Had he decided to embrace fatherhood? And what did that mean for her? Was he going to ask her to marry him again?

Carrie stood up abruptly, in case any of those questions tumbled out of her mouth. 'If that's all? I should get back to work. You have that drinks event at the end of the week.'

'Very well.'

Carrie went to take the tray but Massimo said, 'Leave it. I'll bring it back.'

Before, Carrie would have argued, but now she just

left. She closed the door behind her and stood against it for a moment. She looked down at her hand. It was trembling. Her whole body was tingling. She felt sensitive.

Already there were changes happening. Her waist thickening and her breasts feeling fuller. Had Massimo noticed? Did she want him to notice?

No. That side of their relationship was well and truly over.

It was time to move on and make the best of their new situation.

A few hours later Carrie was lying back on a clinic bed in a very plush private practice. They were briefly alone while the radiographer went to get something. Massimo had changed into a fresh suit. He looked clean-shaven. Carrie's head was suddenly filled with lurid images of Massimo in the shower, naked, with water sluicing over his hard muscles...one in particular.

She wanted to scowl at him for automatically turning her into a hormonal mess on his return. She felt frumpy and lumpen. She *was* a lot thicker in the waist now. More than she remembered being at this stage the first time around.

The worst thing, though, was that she had to admit that the last six weeks had felt very hollow without him. The world had gone from Technicolor to a sort of grey. At night it had been the worst, when she'd wake sweating after a particularly vivid dream, her whole body aching for satisfaction.

She missed him. She missed sex with him.

The radiographer came back in and bustled around Carrie, lifting up her top to spread gel on her belly.

Before Carrie was fully prepared, a loud, rhythmic *thump-thump* filled the room. She went very still as the woman moved the wand over her belly.

'That's a nice strong heartbeat and— Oh, my word...'

Carrie tensed. 'What is it?' She couldn't make out what she was seeing on the screen.

Massimo stepped forward, 'Is everything okay?'

The radiographer looked at Massimo and then at Carrie and smiled beatifically. 'Everything is absolutely fine, but I need to tell you that you're not having just one baby—you're having twins.'

Carrie didn't remember much of what had happened after that—only that the shock she'd felt had been mirrored on Massimo's face. He'd looked as if he'd been punched in the gut.

He was driving them back to the house now, and she might have feared he was in too much shock to drive, but they weren't moving fast in the traffic.

Carrie looked blindly out of the window. She didn't take in the twinkling colourful lights everywhere that indicated Christmas was just around the corner.

She held a print from the scan in her hands. It clearly showed two fig-sized shapes.

Massimo broke the heavy silence. 'There are no twins in my family that I know of.'

Carrie looked at him. His face was in shadow. She didn't want to see his expression.

She felt defensive. 'Mine either. Except,' she had to

concede reluctantly, 'there could be, because I don't know my father's side at all really.'

Massimo said nothing for a long moment, and Carrie could imagine that he must be thinking how distasteful it was that the mother of his children should come from such a sordid background.

Eventually he said, 'I can understand your aversion to marriage. You haven't had the best examples.'

Feeling even more defensive now, Carrie said, 'I could say the same of you.'

'It wasn't a criticism. It was an observation. I'm not a snob, Carrie. My brother and I grew up with silver spoons in our mouths but that didn't protect us from the dysfunction of our family.'

Carrie rubbed at her head. 'Sorry... I'm still in shock.'

Mercifully Massimo was pulling into the forecourt of the house now. Carrie got out. He met her at the front door.

'We need to talk about this. It changes everything.'

Carrie's head thumped. 'Can we talk tomorrow? I'm quite tired.'

Under the light of the porch Massimo looked forbidding, and as if he might refuse, but then he said, 'Fine—tomorrow morning. You're taking the day off tomorrow.'

'But I—'

'No arguments.'

Feeling like a petulant teenager, Carrie went into the house and escaped to her private suite of rooms. She paced back and forth, her arms around her midriff, as if that could contain the lingering shock at what they'd just discovered.

Not one baby. Two babies. Twins.

For a moment Carrie felt absurdly emotional when she thought of losing her first baby and the awful grief she'd felt. Maybe now she was being given another chance.

She felt absurdly protective of these tiny beings that were only just forming. She thought of what Massimo had said: *'This changes everything.'* No. He was wrong. It changed nothing. If anything, knowing there was more at stake now only made it even more important for her to make sure she wasn't railroaded into anything. Massimo, in spite of his family history, was undoubtedly thinking of marriage again.

But she wasn't weak and she wasn't vulnerable— not any more. She was strong and she could stand on her own two feet.

In his office, Massimo couldn't get Carrie's face out of his head—the way she'd looked just now under the porch light. Her eyes had been huge pools of sage-green. Shadows underneath. And she was so pale. The sun-kissed glow from their trip to South America was long gone.

When they'd returned to New York from Brazil Massimo had known he wasn't ready to let her go. He'd actually been considering setting her up in London in her own place. Extending their relationship.

That was one of the reasons he'd felt so exposed when she'd announced her pregnancy. It was as if she'd known and had the trump card to secure her future. But he had to concede now that he hadn't been thinking clearly. Her insistence since then on maintaining her independence was not just for show.

In any case she would have his protection for life now. She was the mother of his child...*children*. He felt slightly light-headed at that thought as it sank in again.

Twins. Two babies. Not one. Two. A ready-made family.

Except Carrie didn't want them to be a family.

And what did he want?

He wanted something he wasn't even ready to name. Was it out of that well-ingrained sense of responsibility? Or was it more?

Something very fragile was unfurling inside him. The possibility of something he'd never considered before because he'd ruled it out so long ago after losing Ricardo. *Love.*

He couldn't keep pretending that what he felt for Carrie was a fleeting thing, or just physical. It was more... and it was deeper.

A sense of resolve filled Massimo's chest. It was happening whether he liked it or not. A family. And even though it terrified him he wanted it. He wanted the chance to live a different life. To have it all.

All he had to do was convince Carrie that there simply was no other option but for them to unite. In every sense of the word. He wouldn't settle for anything less.

CHAPTER EIGHT

'MERRY CHRISTMAS!'

'Merry Christmas.'

Carrie smiled at the departing guest who was weaving a little unsteadily to a car on the forecourt. As soon as she closed the door, the smile slid from her face.

She put a hand to the small of her back to soothe the slight ache there. She'd been on her feet all day, helping to prepare for Massimo's legendary Christmas party. Always a fixture on the London social scene, it was the last hurrah for everyone before Christmas Eve the next day.

She felt constricted in her black shirt and trousers. Soon she would have to stop just buying bigger sizes and invest in some actual maternity wear. Maybe even start wearing dresses.

She was still keeping her pregnancy from the rest of the staff, but she'd noticed a few looks lately. With twins, she was definitely bigger than she would be in a regular pregnancy, and she was approaching four months—almost halfway.

She was exhausted from avoiding Massimo for the last couple of weeks.

The morning after the scan he'd been called away on urgent business—something to do with a charitable fund accused of corruption in Bangkok. Ominously, before he'd left, he'd told her that they'd talk when he got back.

Since he'd come home she'd gone to bed early every night, had volunteered to run all the errands that meant going into town, and had made sure she was otherwise generally occupied.

But the way he'd been looking at her tonight at the party told her the jig was up. Everywhere she'd looked, he'd been there. At one point during the evening she'd taken a full tray from one of the waiters and within seconds Massimo had been there, taking it from her and handing it to someone else.

He'd said in a low voice, 'This is ridiculous, Carrie. You do not serve. You supervise. And I've changed my mind. *This*—' here he'd gestured to her and then the room in general '—is not working for me.'

The intensity of his gaze had stopped her from saying anything and he'd melted back into the crowd— well, as much as someone like him *could* melt, when he stood head and shoulders above almost everyone else.

She went and stood at one of the doors, looking into the party. It was winding down now. She didn't know how he did it, but Massimo had some magical way of letting everyone know that it was time to go home. There were never the scenes of debauchery here that she imagined he must have witnessed as a child.

The butler came and stood beside her. 'You were up earlier than me today, Carrie,' he said. 'You take off. I can look after things from here.'

She looked at Dave. 'Are you sure? The events manager is standing by, to make sure the last guests get away without delay and the initial clean-up has started.'

He nodded. 'It's all sorted. You head off.'

The thought of escaping Massimo's brooding gaze and their inevitable conversation was too much to resist. Carrie slipped away, and when she got to her room she ran a bath, stripping off and sliding into it with a groan of thanks.

She put her hands on her burgeoning belly. It felt hard. Her breasts were definitely bigger too, the areolae changing colour. She felt…ripe. Full of something she couldn't quite understand. An edgy sense of restlessness.

Whenever she'd caught Massimo looking at her this evening she'd felt a very unwelcome jolt of awareness, as if he could see right through her clothes to the naked flesh underneath.

One hand drifted to her breast, cupping its weight. She let her fingers graze the nipple and gasped out loud at the immediate sensation. She'd been feeling sensitive, but had had no idea just how close to the surface it was.

The edginess she'd been feeling dissipated for the first time in weeks. Trapping her nipple between two fingers was inducing a delicious feeling of tension. Acting on pure instinct, she put her other hand between her legs, where she could feel the slippery evidence of her very obvious desire.

Had it been brought on just from watching Massimo from across the room? Or had it been building since the last time she'd slept with him?

The thought of never sleeping with him again made something reckless move through Carrie, and she pressed her hand against herself—hard. It wasn't enough. She slipped two fingers inside herself and her back arched at the sensation. She started to move, desperately chasing the coiling tension deep inside, as her other hand squeezed her breast. She imagined it was Massimo's big hand between her legs, his fingers filling her as he urged her to *Come for me, Carrie... That's it...come on...let go...*

She did—in a helpless rush of undulating pleasure.

It took her a moment to realise she could hear knocking, and a voice.

'Carrie?'

Massimo.

Carrie panicked in a wave of hot mortification. Had she literally conjured him up out of her fervid imagination?

She called out, 'I'm in the bath…give me a minute.'

She cursed him as she got out and dried herself roughly, before pulling on a voluminous robe. Her body was still pulsating. She was red in the face. She put her hair up in a rough knot. She cursed him again, and went to open the door.

He was standing on the other side, bow-tie undone, top button open. She would have thought him every inch the disreputable rake, if she didn't know that he was actually quite serious and conscientious.

That only made her heart squeeze. *Weak heart.*

She pulled the lapels of her robe together like a virgin maiden. 'I was having a bath. Is everything all right? Dave said he'd look after the last of the party...'

Massimo waved a hand. 'It's fine...they're all gone now.'

Carrie was glad he couldn't see through to her skin, where her blood was still pulsing. Seeing him here like this in a tuxedo so soon after she'd just been—

'What can I help you with?' she blurted out, trying not to remember what she'd just been doing.

He said, 'It's Christmas Eve tomorrow.'

Carrie blinked. 'Yes, it is.'

She usually spent Christmas alone in her suite. A couple of times other staff had invited her for dinner, but she'd made up an excuse. Christmas wasn't an especially significant time of the year for her. It had always just been her and her mother, and she'd learnt very early that she shouldn't ask for things that made her mother feel she had to work harder to provide.

Her husband hadn't particularly enjoyed it either, and so Carrie had channelled any childish Christmas fantasies into her love of Christmas movies. Since his death, and losing her baby, she'd seen spending Christmas by herself as a sort of penance.

'What are you doing on Christmas Day?' asked Massimo.

'I have the day off.'

'I know you do. What are you doing?'

'Taking it easy.'

'I've given all the staff the day off.'

'You usually do,' Carrie pointed out.

Massimo was rarely here for Christmas himself—he'd usually be abroad. Christmas and New Year were high season for parties and philanthropy.

'Well, it looks like it'll just be the two of us here, then.'

Carrie was suspicious. 'I won't disturb you.'

'It would be very sad if we were both alone in the house on Christmas Day and didn't even share dinner together.'

'There's no one to cook it.'

She could cook it. She wouldn't mind cooking it. But cooking an intimate Christmas dinner for Massimo would be both far too seductive and terrifying.

'Chef is going to leave an idiot-proof Christmas dinner. All I have to do is heat it up for us.'

'Us.'

'Yes, *us*. I'm not taking no for an answer.'

He'd turned and walked away before Carrie could formulate a response.

After all her successful efforts to avoid Massimo, how had it happened that she was now going to be spending Christmas with him?

Feeling ridiculously nervous, Carrie made her way to meet Massimo on Christmas Day, late afternoon. Sounds emerged from the kitchen. The loud clatter of metal on tiles and a voluble curse.

Carrie couldn't help a smile and bit her lip as she stood in the doorway and surveyed the scene. Massimo had his back to her. He was wearing a white shirt and black trousers, and he was holding up a saucepan and looking at it as if he'd never seen one before. Which he might well not have, up close.

As if sensing her presence, he turned around with a rueful expression on his face. His gaze swept her up and down, and to Carrie's mortification she felt the heat of it, when she knew there was no heat intended. As soon as she'd told him of her pregnancy, any desire he'd had for her had died a death.

She regretted picking out the soft jersey dress in dark green. Pairing it with tights and high heels. She felt too conspicuously dressed up, and the material of the dress felt too clingy. Especially around her burgeoning midriff, which seemed to be going through a growth spurt.

She regretted leaving her hair down too—had she done that subconsciously? Was her own brain trying to betray her? It was too late in any case to do anything about it.

'Are you having some trouble?' she asked, walking into the kitchen.

Sounding a little defensive, he said, 'I'm not sure which pan to use to heat the gravy.'

Carrie walked over and opened a drawer and pulled out a small one. 'This one should do.'

There was a piece of paper on the counter-top with a list of things to do in sequential order to prepare the meal.

Carrie took pity on Massimo and put on an apron after handing him one. 'Let me help.'

They worked in a surprisingly companionable silence as they moved back and forth, taking the food

Chef had prepared out of its packaging and putting it into the oven to heat.

Once everything was heating, Massimo said, 'You can go upstairs. I'll bring the food once it's ready.'

Carrie thought of the dining room and imagined them sitting there at the table, with low lighting, while a fire burned in the fireplace and the skies darkened outside. Far too intimate.

'I don't mind eating here. It'd be a lot easier.'

Massimo said, 'It's no trouble at all. I've laid the fire upstairs. All it needs is to be lit.'

The tone of his voice brooked no argument. So Carrie took off the apron and said, 'Whatever you prefer. I'll light the fire, then.'

She escaped upstairs and found the informal dining room table already laid and prepared for dinner with plates and cutlery and condiments. A bottle of wine sat open on the table, and a choice of non-alcoholic drinks. Thoughtful. An impeccably decorated Christmas tree twinkled in the corner of the room.

She found matches and lit the fire. As if to mock her, it blazed immediately and cheerfully in the hearth, sending out delicious heat. She stood before it, feeling a little dazed at all that had happened in the last few months and by the fact that she was pregnant. With twins.

She put a hand on her belly. She couldn't feel any movement yet, apart from the odd, very light fluttering sensation.

She sat down in a chair beside the fire, kicking off

her shoes, and curled her legs up, mesmerised by the flames and not even noticing her eyelids getting heavy.

Massimo came up to the dining room with the first tray laden with their Christmas dinner. He stopped on the threshold when he saw Carrie asleep in a chair by the fire.

He put down the tray silently and looked at her. Her hair was tumbling over her shoulders. He'd like to think she'd left it down on purpose, but the way she looked at him these days—so warily—made it not likely.

He let his gaze rove over her body, greedy to see it revealed under the soft material of the dress. He couldn't stop his own body's helpless and wanton reaction to seeing the evidence of her body growing riper and fuller with his child. With his *children*.

Once again he was taken aback that the dominant force of emotions moving through him wasn't negative. It was wonder, trepidation and an urge to protect, mixed with a sense of possessiveness. And a feeling that his fears of destructive genes being passed down was just that—a fear.

He'd allowed himself to hope that perhaps, with a new generation, he could make things right. Create a healthy and functional family. But for that he'd need Carrie. Body, heart and soul. He knew he wouldn't settle for less.

Her insistence that she had to keep working here as a means to stay close and let Massimo be involved in the pregnancy couldn't go on for much longer—if at all.

If he had to wage all-out war to get Carrie to see sense then he would. And he would play as dirty as he needed to.

At that moment, as if she sensed Massimo's intense focus on her, her eyes fluttered open. He noticed she was unguarded for a moment, and that something flared in her eyes when she saw him, but then it was gone. As if she'd brought down shutters.

She still wanted him.

His blood leapt. If she still wanted him they were halfway there.

She sat up, looking flustered, cheeks pink. 'How long was I asleep?'

'Not long.'

Carrie stood up and came over to him, helping take the plates off the tray. 'It smells good.'

'Alas, I can take no credit at all.'

'Heating food isn't without its challenges.'

'I'll take that as a compliment,' Massimo said dryly.

Carrie watched Massimo walk out to go and get the rest of the food. She still felt a little fuzzy. She put the plates on the table and tried not to think about how it had felt to wake up and find Massimo watching her so intently.

She'd thought she was dreaming...until she'd realised she wasn't.

Massimo returned with the rest of the food.

Carrie was finding it hard to shake the slightly dreamy feeling brought on by her nap. With the fire lit and darkness falling outside, the intimacy of the scenario was exactly as she'd feared. But she couldn't seem to drum up the energy to care too much.

She sat down and Massimo served up a delicious traditional roast with all the trimmings.

After a few mouthfuls, Carrie put down her knife and fork. 'I wouldn't have thought you were a big fan of Christmas—you're not usually here.'

Massimo made a face and took a sip of wine. He put down the glass. 'I can take it or leave it. Christmas when I was growing up was chaotic, so I've never really had the traditional experience.' Almost as an afterthought, he said, 'Except for once.'

'Oh?' Carrie had to admit she was intrigued by any glimpse into Massimo's early life.

'Well, Christmas with my parents was all or nothing. They either lavished us with gifts when they were organised and had remembered, or we were left with the nanny while they went on holiday. But one year the nanny couldn't stay with us, so we went to a schoolfriend's house to spend it with his family.'

'What was that like?'

'A revelation. For the first time in our lives Ric and I witnessed a functional family. A loving family. Who celebrated Christmas the same way every year. Very simple, nothing fancy—the boy was at our school on a scholarship—and yet when it came to it his parents were the ones who offered to take us in for the Christmas holidays.'

'Did you enjoy it?'

'It was a little unsettling—like being an alien beamed

down from another planet and learning how to behave like normal people. Playing games. Watching movies. There was none of the high-octane glamour and chaos that we usually witnessed. I think Ric discovered drugs for the first time at one of our parents' parties.'

Carrie couldn't help feeling a pang at the thought of two young boys feeling so lost in a normal situation that most people took for granted.

She said, 'Christmas when I was growing up was just me and my mother. We didn't have enough money for this kind of feast, but she always tried her best so that we'd have some kind of treat. And we'd watch movies. She loved all the old classics, like *It's A Wonderful Life* and *Miracle on 34th Street.*'

'You miss her?'

Carrie nodded, avoiding Massimo's eye. 'She was all I had. She was wonderful.'

'You were lucky to know a mother's love. Our mother was a kind person, but she didn't have the ability to be responsible. She'd been totally pampered as a child, and yet her own parents had farmed her out to nannies and boarding schools. She literally didn't know what to do with us. And her fragile emotional state meant she was very susceptible to alcohol and drugs. Our father's philandering only made things worse.'

Carrie looked at Massimo. He was staring into his wine glass.

She said, 'That must have been tough.'

He shrugged. 'It was all we knew.'

He looked at her and Carrie was caught by his dark

gaze, turning golden in the low lights and the fire in the background.

He said, 'You must have been young when you married.'

'I was eighteen.'

Massimo made a faint whistling sound. 'That's *young*.'

'My mother had recently died. I was feeling a little…lost. Vulnerable. I was an easy target for someone who recognised weakness and wanted to exploit it and exert control.'

'You weren't weak. You were grieving.'

Carrie let his words fall into that place inside her where she'd punished herself for so long. They didn't sting. They were like a balm.

'I let him in and he took advantage. That's why I won't marry again. I don't trust myself not to let it happen again. The thought is…terrifying.'

'So you'd prefer our children to grow up with separate parents?'

Carrie tensed. 'You'd have access. Separate parents has to be healthier than a marriage made for the sake of the children. I could keep—'

Massimo cut her off. 'Do not say you could keep working here. It's not feasible Carrie. Not any more. You're already showing a little.'

Carrie was feeling claustrophobic. 'The staff don't have to find out the babies are yours.'

The sudden tension in the room crackled.

Massimo stood up. 'These babies are the heirs to the Linden fortune and a legacy that stretches back to the Middle Ages. You'd deny them that?'

Instinctively Carrie put her hand on her belly, as if to shield the babies from Massimo's terrifying words. 'I… I hadn't thought about it like that, to be honest.'

She really hadn't. She'd known it was there in the ether, like some existential thing she would have to deal with eventually. And she'd also known deep down that she couldn't keep going as she was. Massimo wouldn't stand for it. He was a proud man.

He started to pace back and forth, the delicious Christmas dinner forgotten. '*This* is why we need to talk—but you've turned avoiding me into an Olympic sport.'

Carrie said, a little weakly, 'We're talking now.'

'Because we are literally the only two people in the house.'

When he said that a different kind of tension filled the air. Something that was more charged.

Carrie put it down to her imagination. Since that other evening in the bath she'd felt ridiculously aware of everything.

'Look,' he said, running a hand through his hair, 'we do need to discuss this properly. Our children deserve security and stability.'

And two parents who love each other, thought Carrie, surprised as that assertion slid into her consciousness.

Obviously two parents who loved each other would be the ideal. But, having not experienced that herself—and nor had Massimo—it would have to be good enough that they loved their children.

Massimo sat down again. 'Why did you stay with your husband?' he asked bluntly.

Carrie balked a little. But then, 'At first it was because he charmed me and flattered me. He made me feel safe and secure. Cared for.'

Loved.

But that had been her mistake. It hadn't been love. It had been an obsessive need to coerce and control someone.

'And then…?'

'When I realised it was destructive and potentially physically dangerous for me, I told him I wanted to leave him. But then I discovered I was pregnant. I felt conflicted. On the one hand I knew I had to leave, for my own safety and sanity, but on the other hand I had grown up without a father, and I didn't want that for my own child. That's why we were having a row in the car…he'd sensed my turmoil over what to do.'

'That was a terrible price to pay and it wasn't your fault.'

Carrie looked at Massimo. 'I know… It took a long time to forgive myself, though. I think you can understand that.'

Massimo's jaw clenched. 'I don't know if I can ever forgive myself for not being stricter with Ric.'

Carrie reached out. 'Mass—'

But he'd stood up again. 'Let me clear this and I'll bring up dessert.'

Carrie stood up too. 'I can do it.'

But he was already stacking the plates and taking them out.

Carrie wandered back over to the fire and threw a couple of logs on, making the flames jump and hiss. She knew Massimo was right. They did need to talk about the future and how it would look. She knew that under no circumstances did she want marriage. Not after her last experience. Even though she had to concede that Massimo had proved over and over again that he was not like her husband.

She trusted him.

She cared about Massimo—she couldn't deny it. Cared deeply. He'd not only been her lover, he'd been a friend.

But something was holding her back from investigating just how deep those feelings went.

Fear.

She'd believed herself in love before, and she'd been so wrong that she didn't trust herself to know what love was. If she named what she was feeling as love, then Massimo would use it as an excuse to make her agree to marriage. And if she agreed to the marriage and she was the only one in love it would destroy her all over again.

You're a coward, whispered a little voice.

There was a sound as Massimo reappeared with dessert. A choice of traditional Christmas pudding or crumble. Tea and coffee.

Carrie sat down again and chose some crumble, focusing on it very intently so that she could avoid looking at Massimo.

'You've turned avoiding me into an Olympic sport.'

She couldn't imagine any of his previous lovers avoiding him as she'd been doing.

Thinking of them made her feel spiky. She hadn't even thought about what would happen if he did marry. Someone else. The prospect made her feel a little breathless.

Almost accusingly, she said, 'For someone who never wanted to marry or have a family you seem pretty sanguine about it.'

Massimo took a sip of coffee. Carrie couldn't help but notice his big hands. It had been so long since she'd felt his hands on her. She ached to be touched...

She scowled inwardly. Pregnancy hormones. Apparently in the second trimester it was common to feel... aroused.

'It's one thing to take a position on a hypothetical situation,' he said. 'But when that situation is no longer hypothetical and becomes a reality, it's a very different thing.'

'What are you saying?'

'I'm saying that I might not have wanted this, but now that it's happening I find that I'm not as averse to it as I thought. I want to do things differently. Our children deserve a better life than I experienced or you experienced. We can give that to them.'

We.

Carrie's head was starting to throb a little. She said, 'Can we agree to talk about this again in the New Year?'

Massimo looked as if he wanted to disagree, but eventually he said, 'Fine.' And then, 'I have something for you.'

Carrie watched as Massimo went to the Christmas tree in the corner of the room and picked up a small box. Her heart thumped. Surely he wouldn't...? Flashbacks of her husband giving her a small velvet box made her feel queasy.

Massimo handed it to her. She took it reluctantly. She was afraid to open it.

'You look terrified. It's not horrible, I promise.'

Carrie glanced at Massimo and then back down at the box. She took a deep breath and opened it. And was immediately filled with a mixture of relief and—more worryingly—disappointment. It was a stunning pair of diamond drop earrings, glinting in the light.

She looked at Massimo. 'They're beautiful but they're too much.'

When he spoke his tone was dry. 'I've never given jewellery to a woman before. But you're going to be the mother of my children.'

Relief flooded her to know she was the first woman he'd given anything like this to. 'Well, thank you, but you really didn't need to.'

'Try them on.'

The air became charged again. Carrie cursed her hormones, telling herself it was only natural that he would want to see them on her. She took them out of the box carefully and slipped them into her ears.

Massimo's gaze narrowed on her. Carrie felt heat rising.

'They suit you.'

'Thank you.' And then, before she could make a fool of herself, Carrie said, 'I have something for you too.'

She got up and went over to the tree, where she'd put his gift the previous day. She'd panicked, realising she had to give him something.

She picked it up, suddenly feeling incredibly nervous. At the time it hadn't felt like a particularly intimate thing, but now, in this cocoon-like room, it felt like an unexploded bomb.

She handed it to Massimo before she lost her nerve, saying, 'I didn't know what to get you… I mean, what do you get the man who has everything?'

He looked up at her. 'You really think I have everything?'

Carrie was taken aback at the bleak tone in his voice.

She sat down again. 'Well, I guess…materially, yes…'

He was taking off the pretty golden bow and pulling back the paper.

She babbled nervously. 'I just had an idea…maybe I'm totally off the mark…'

Oh, God. He was going to hate it.

But Massimo had taken off the paper now, and was looking down at the simple silver picture frame. His voice when he spoke was a little hoarse, and he didn't look at her. 'Where did you find this picture?'

'I found it on the internet. I remembered seeing it a long time ago, when I'd just started working here and wanted to find out more about you…my boss. It always struck me as such a happy picture, and I realised I hadn't seen it anywhere here.'

'That's because it was taken by a paparazzo.'

The picture had been taken after a motor race that Ricardo had won. He had his arm around Massimo and they were looking at each other, both smiling. Massimo had an affectionately exasperated expression on his face and Ricardo looked as if he'd just said something cheeky.

It seemed to encapsulate everything Massimo had told her about how he felt about his brother and the great love and bond between them.

Massimo touched the glass with one finger.

Carrie said nervously, 'Look, if I've intruded…'

Massimo glanced at her and said dryly, 'I think that horse has bolted now, don't you?'

She blushed. She was sitting here with the evidence of that statement in her belly.

As if hearing her thoughts, Massimo's gaze travelled down to her midriff.

'Can you feel anything yet?'

Carrie shook her head. 'Another couple of weeks.'

He looked back up at her face and put the picture down. He said, 'Thank you for that…it's very special.'

'You're welcome.'

Carrie didn't seem to be able to break eye contact with Massimo… Afraid he'd see her desire laid bare in her eyes, on her face, she stood up and said, 'Thank you for going to all this effort to make Christmas special. It was nice. But I think I'll head for bed.'

Massimo stood too. Surprising her, he said, 'Look at your earrings in the mirror.'

The air was charged again. Carrie's blood felt heavy in her veins. 'I can do that in my room.'

'Humour me?'

He took her hand—their first real physical contact since she'd told him she was pregnant. Her legs turned to jelly. He led her over to where there was a mirror on the wall above a small table.

He placed her in front of him. She looked so small with Massimo towering behind her. She couldn't look at herself.

He said, 'May I?'

She didn't even know what he was asking until she felt him draw her hair back. He let his fingers linger, lightly massaging her scalp. It was the most decadent, blissful thing Carrie had ever felt. She wanted to melt like liquid back into Massimo's strong frame and—

She stiffened and looked at herself in the mirror. Hair down and tousled. Cheeks pink. Eyes too bright. She could see her nipples, hard and thrusting against the material of her dress. The diamonds in her ears glittered.

And Massimo was watching her. Reading all those glaring signs. He was playing with her.

She pulled away and Massimo's hands dropped. She tried to smooth her hair into some semblance of tidiness.

'What are you doing?' she asked.

'I still want you, Carrie.'

She took a step back, as if he'd physically pushed her. 'No, you don't.'

He made a face. 'Oh, I can assure you I do. I've never stopped wanting you.'

'But when I told you I was pregnant you agreed that whatever we'd had was over.'

'I was in shock. Angry. After a lifetime of maintaining a healthy distrust of everyone around me I felt like I'd been the biggest fool, falling for the oldest trick in the book.'

That still stung. 'And now?'

'I know you're not like that, Carrie. I knew it then. I just couldn't undo a lifetime's teaching in twenty-four hours.'

'So you trust me?'

Massimo nodded. 'Yes, but even now it's not easy for me to admit it.'

Carrie appreciated his honesty.

He said, 'But you don't trust me.'

She balked at that. 'I... I do.'

And she knew she did...but deep down there was a place where doubt and fear lingered.

Massimo shook his head. He took a step towards her. She could feel his heat.

'No, there's something holding you back,' he said, 'And after your experiences I can't blame you. But I do still want you, Carrie. These last couple of months have been the longest of my life...wanting you. I think that if you can come to trust me, and knowing that we want each other, we have as good a chance as anyone in making a marriage work.'

She opened her mouth but he put up a hand, stopping her from talking.

'We certainly have a better chance than our parents had. I'm just asking that you give this...*us*...a chance.'

Carrie had been about to refute his claim that they wanted each other, but she was glad now that she hadn't spoken that lie, because he would have laughed in her face.

But how on earth was she going to cope now that she knew he did still want her?

CHAPTER NINE

Two weeks later

CARRIE GROANED AND stretched her back. It was getting harder and harder to hide her growing bump. She'd noticed staff looking at her and whispering behind her back. And whenever she had dealings with Massimo their last conversation hung in the air between them, as pregnant as her belly.

Her whole body ached to be touched. The air crackled with live electricity whenever they were close.

It was embarrassing.

He was growing more brooding, matching the inclement January weather outside. Lowering grey skies and a bitter chill. Winter had come and it was here in Massimo's townhouse.

Carrie knew she was running out of time. Massimo was right. She couldn't keep working here as if nothing had changed. She had to face up to her future and decide what was best for her and the babies.

But not today. It was Sunday morning and she had the day off. She planned on spending it hiding from the world, from Massimo, and all of the things she should be thinking about.

She planned on paying homage to her mother and binge-watching all the old movies they'd loved.

She was dressed in leisurewear—joggers and a sweatshirt. She stopped in front of a mirror and pulled her sweatshirt up to reveal the very distinct bump of her belly. Without her uniform and trying to suck herself in, it was very noticeable now. In another month she would have a scan that would reveal the sex of the babies—all being well. Making this even more of a reality.

The back of her neck prickled and she tensed. In the mirror she saw a reflection of Massimo in the doorway. She was caught for a moment, wondering if she was imagining him there, like she imagined him far too much in her dreams, and also when she was awake.

But he didn't disappear.

She whirled around, dropping the sweatshirt again to cover her belly. 'Excuse me?'

Massimo looked unrepentant. 'I did knock. You didn't hear me.'

That was very possible. Carrie felt exposed. And shabby. And then she noticed that Massimo was wearing faded jeans and a woollen sweater. He hardly ever dressed down.

'Was there something you wanted?'

He looked at her and she felt the zing of his silent response. Her cheeks grew hot. Then he said, 'Yes, I want to show you something, but it's out of the city. It's a drive. Will you come with me?'

Carrie automatically wanted to say no, but she felt

as if she'd been running for a long time, and she just wanted to give in and let someone else take over.

'Okay.'

Massimo looked shocked. 'You'll come?'

'Yes.'

'You might want to change into something warmer—it's cold out.'

She'd heard snow being forecast on the radio earlier. 'When do you want to go?' she asked.

'As soon as you're ready.'

'Give me fifteen minutes.'

He left, and Carrie slipped out of her casual clothes and picked out a pair of maternity jeans, which she paired with thick socks and an undershirt and a fleece top. She pulled her hair back, and then at the last moment a rogue part of her made her leave it down.

Because Massimo liked it down.

She made a face at herself. But she left it down.

She went downstairs to meet Massimo and took a sheepskin jacket out of the closet. She was effectively swaddled. No chance of anyone noticing the bump.

But Massimo had just seen it.

He appeared then, as if conjured from her thoughts. He pulled on a warm jacket too, and said, 'Ready?'

She nodded and followed him out to his SUV. He was driving. He opened the passenger door and she got in. She watched him walk around the front and sighed a little at the way he moved with such effortless athletic grace.

They were silent as Massimo drove through the relatively quiet streets and then took one of London's main arteries out of the city. Carrie saw signs for Surrey.

Massimo asked, 'Aren't you curious about where we're going?'

No, because that would mean initiating conversation.

Carrie said, 'I like surprises.'

'Fair enough.'

The skies were even lower now, and that particular leaden colour that signalled snow. But Carrie wasn't unduly worried. Even if it did snow, it most likely wouldn't settle.

After about an hour, Massimo drove through a picturesque village and then slowed down on the other side as they drove alongside an old wall. After a few minutes he turned into a wide gateway. The iron gates opened automatically and he drove up a long and winding drive, surrounded by nothing as far as the eye could see except rolling hills and bare trees, lush fields even in winter.

Carrie sat up straight when a very imposing and frankly intimidatingly large house—no, surely a castle?—came into view ahead of them, between two long lines of manicured bushes.

'Where are we?'

Massimo's voice was tight when he answered. 'The family seat, Linden Hall.'

Ah. Understanding dawned. He wanted to show her exactly what their children were going to inherit.

At first glance the building was almost pretty, but Carrie shivered slightly. All the windows and the two imposing wings on either end of the building gave it a slightly less pretty edge.

Massimo drove the car right up to the front door. But 'door' was too ineffectual a word for what this massive entrance really was. He got out and the door opened to reveal a relatively normal-looking older couple, who were smiling at Massimo.

Carrie was surprised to see him greet them warmly, with kisses. She got out, curious.

He turned to her and said, 'Carrie, I'd like you to meet Sheila and Tom Fields. They live here and care-take the estate for me.'

Of course. Carrie had heard their names over the years, but she'd never met them.

She moved forward and shook their hands, smiling shyly. 'I can imagine that's some undertaking.'

Tom chuckled. 'Oh, yes! We have four hundred acres here, not to mention the house, but we have a dedicated team to help us.'

Sheila smiled warmly. 'Please, come in out of the cold. We've prepared a light lunch.'

Carrie's stomach rumbled embarrassingly. She saw Sheila's shrewd eyes drop to her midriff and widen slightly. Carrie looked down to see her coat hanging open and the unmistakable bulge of her growing bump on view. She smiled weakly.

They were ushered in and taken straight down to a massive state-of-the-art kitchen that still managed to be warm and homely. While Tom was talking estate business to Massimo, Carrie went to help Sheila with the lunch.

The older woman said, 'So you're Massimo's Lon-

don housekeeper. We never really go up to town, but
we have heard of you.'

Carrie went still at the thought of what Massimo
might have said. The woman seemed to take pity on her.

'Don't worry, he hasn't said a thing. I'm putting two
and two together and probably coming up with six. But
all I know is that Massimo has never brought anyone
here, and unless you're coming to take over our jobs...'

Carrie smiled weakly again. 'No, your jobs are safe.'

'Well, then,' Sheila said, with a twinkle in her eye.

But she didn't elaborate on that, and Carrie was
grateful as she helped her to set out soup and bread
and some salad.

After lunch, and a very genial chat, Carrie knew she
liked the couple. They were down to earth and straightforward.

Massimo stood up. 'I'm going to show Carrie
around.'

Tom stood up too. 'Okay, but maybe not outside for
now. I don't like the look of that sky.'

Neither did Carrie when Massimo led her back into
the entrance hall and she saw the vast mass of slate-
grey outside. She shivered again.

'Cold? Do you want me to get your coat?'

Carrie shook her head. 'No, I'm fine.'

'Come on—let me give you the tour.'

Carrie dutifully followed Massimo through vast reception rooms, ballrooms, dining rooms, and then upstairs to more bedrooms than she could count. It was
dizzying.

When he took her up to the top level, where the servants' quarters used to be, Carrie stopped in the middle of a corridor. He stopped too, and looked at her.

She put her hands out. 'Okay, I get it, Massimo. Consider your point made. Our children stand to inherit one of the country's finest estates.'

Massimo leant against a wall and folded his arms. 'I've always hated this place. I had actually intended donating it to the National Trust, ensuring that all profits made would go to charity.'

'Oh.'

'But in light of our current situation I've decided to hold off. I will open it to the public, though, to help Sheila and Tom with the upkeep. And again any profits can go to charity. But I'll leave it up to our children to decide what they want to do with it.'

Our children.

Those words sent far too many conflicting emotions through her.

Carrie saw something out of the corner of her eye and looked out of the window. She gasped.

Massimo looked too, and cursed softly. He said, 'Come on, we need to get back to Tom and Sheila.'

Carrie was still mesmerised by the fact that in the space of time it had taken them to walk through the house—admittedly it was vast—the world had turned white outside. A thick blanket of snow now covered everything and it was still falling heavily.

She hurried after Massimo and found him in the hall with Sheila and Tom, their coats on. They looked worried.

Tom was saying, 'The forecast isn't good. They're

already saying the small roads are blocked. If you don't have to go back, I'd advise staying the night. They're saying it'll clear tomorrow.'

Carrie immediately wanted to protest, but she bit her lip.

Sheila came over. 'I'm sorry we have to leave you here, but the kitchen is well stocked and Massimo will light some fires. The water is hot—you'll be fine.'

'Where are you going?' asked Carrie. 'Will you be all right?'

'Yes, fine. We live in a cottage on the estate, not far from the house—if we leave now we'll get there safely. Tom can clear the road from there in the morning.'

Carrie didn't want to worry this woman, so she said, 'We'll be fine here. I think a night in a listed mansion can't exactly be considered a hardship.'

The woman smiled, and her eyes shone with genuine warmth as she said conspiratorially, 'I'm so glad Massimo has found someone like *you*, dear. He deserves to be happy.'

The woman was gone with her husband before Carrie could fully absorb that nugget.

When they were gone, driving off in their own sturdy SUV, Massimo put on his coat, saying, 'I need to go and get some supplies for the fires.'

'Do you need help?'

'Not for this. Maybe see what's in the kitchen that we can have for dinner later?'

Carrie watched as he left and got into the car and drove off. The snow was already a few inches high against the tyres. She felt a moment of fear, watching him go out of sight, and the house suddenly seemed huge and ominous around her…as if ghostly eyes were watching her.

She shook it off, telling herself she was being ridiculous, and made her way down to the comforting kitchen.

She was poring over a cookbook when Massimo returned. She tried not to let it show how relieved she was. He was carrying an armload of logs and he was covered in snowflakes.

He put the logs down by the fireplace and started to light it. He did this with an ease that spoke of his doing it many times before.

Carrie said, 'I wouldn't have thought you were used to doing the manual labour around here—weren't you the cossetted heir?'

Massimo made a huffing sound. 'That's what my mother would have preferred, but there was usually so much chaos going on upstairs at any given time that Ric and I used to come down here and do our homework or hang out with the staff.' He stood up and looked around. 'This was always my favourite part of the house. Sheila and Tom weren't living on the estate then, but they were a consistent presence and provided some security—more than the revolving door of nannies.'

Carrie marvelled again at the dark reality of Massimo's supposedly gilded life.

Massimo took off his coat and hung it on the back of the door. 'Do you mind staying here tonight?'

She shrugged. 'Looks like we have no choice. And I can think of worse places to stay.'

As if he couldn't help himself, he came over and

reached out, touching her cheek with a finger. 'You're one a million, you know that?'

His touch was like an electric shock, zinging right into her blood.

Warmth bloomed near her heart.

Around her heart.

In her heart.

She froze inside. *No.* She wasn't ready to allow that thought in.

She pulled down Massimo's hand and stepped back. 'I'm really not.'

Stubble was lining Massimo's jaw. His hair was damp and dishevelled from the snow. Carrie ached for his touch again. To touch him. Wanting him and needing to keep her distance was making her dizzy.

She took another step back and babbled, 'There's the makings of a stew in the pantry and fridge... I've found a nice recipe... I can make that later.'

'Keep resisting, Carrie, for as long as you can. I'm not going anywhere.'

Massimo sauntered back out of the kitchen and Carrie called after him. 'You planned this, didn't you?'

He came back to the doorway and opened his hands out wide. 'I can do a lot of things, Carrie, but even I can't influence the weather.'

He disappeared again and Carrie cursed him.

To take her mind off Massimo and their situation, she put on an apron and started preparing dinner. It was best to keep herself busy.

Carrie looked up at one point and realised that the fire was dying down and it was growing dark outside.

She threw some more logs on the fire and put the stew in the oven.

Wondering where Massimo was, but also reluctant to find him, she wandered upstairs. Massive portraits of the people who must be Massimo's ancestors glared down at her.

She shouldn't be here.

She shouldn't be carrying his child.

Worse, his children.

On an impulse Carrie stuck her tongue out at one particularly glowering dour-looking man.

'I used to do that too.'

Carrie jumped about three feet in the air, her hand over her heart. Massimo was standing in a doorway nearby.

'Sorry, I didn't mean to scare you.'

Carrie looked back at the picture and admitted, 'I can't help but feel they're judging me.'

'You're not the only one. Remember, we were the children of an Italian woman who might have been a countess but was still considered not exactly the best choice of society wife at the time.'

Carrie looked at him. He'd obviously inherited his looks from his mother's side. 'You really did stick out your tongue at them?'

'Yes, just like this.'

And he stuck out his tongue—which immediately made Carrie think of how it had felt on her mouth, in her mouth, on her skin...between her legs.

She blurted out, 'I just came to tell you that the stew should be ready in an hour or so.'

'Lovely, thank you. I'll come down shortly.'

Carrie fled back to the kitchen.

'This is delicious,' Massimo declared when he'd swallowed some of the stew.

'I can't really take any credit. Sheila had the ingredients ready to go—all I did was throw them together.'

The kitchen, in spite of its size, was cosy. The fire crackled in the huge fireplace, sending out comforting warmth.

After they'd eaten in companionable silence for a few minutes, Carrie said, 'I was thinking about some things…'

Massimo put down his cutlery. 'Oh?'

Carrie could see the gleam in his eyes. She said quickly, 'Not that.'

Massimo took a sip of water. 'What, then?'

'About the children. They'll have this huge legacy, of course, but I don't want them to go to a boarding school in the middle of nowhere with posh kids.

'Sorry,' she said then, in case she might have offended him.

'I agree.' Massimo wiped his mouth with a napkin.

Carrie was shocked. 'You do?'

'Boarding school did nothing for me and Ric except teach us how to stand up to bullies who thought we were inferior because we were half-Italian. I'd be happy for the children to go to a day school.'

'Near us?'

Massimo's gaze narrowed on Carrie. '*Us?* So you'll be living with me?'

She cursed herself—she hadn't been thinking. 'Not necessarily, but I would be nearby.'

Massimo looked exasperated. 'Carrie, look—'

Suddenly the lights went out.

Massimo cursed. 'That's the power gone. I guess it was inevitable.'

'What do we do now?'

It was pitch-black except for the firelight.

'Find some torches and candles…they're in a cupboard here.'

He got up and turned on his phone light, found some torches and thick candles.

Carrie took a torch. Its powerful beam lit up the kitchen enough for her to gather the plates and put them in a pile by the sink.

Massimo said, 'If the power is still off in the morning we have a generator we can power up.'

Carrie felt panicky. 'Tom said it was only going to snow tonight.'

'It's just a back-up,' he said. 'There's nothing for it now but to go to bed—it'll soon get cold. I'll go up and light fires in the bedrooms. You wait here.'

Carrie immediately thought of herself, sitting there in the dark, and said, 'No, I'll come with you and help. I don't mind.'

Massimo shrugged. He led her upstairs, his torch lighting their way.

Carrie asked, 'Does this happen a lot?'

'Regularly enough, which is why we have the generator. These days, though, they usually have the power restored within hours. I'm sure it'll be on again by morning.' Then he asked, 'Are you scared of the dark?'

'I'm not overly keen on it...put it that way.'

Her husband had known she hated the dark, and had insisted on turning off every light at night. It had increased Carrie's sense of fear even though he'd never lifted a hand to her.

Massimo took her hand and another one of Carrie's defences wobbled precariously.

They reached the first floor and Massimo opened the door to a massive bedroom. 'You can have this room.'

Carrie knew immediately it must be his. 'I don't mind a smaller one...really.'

He ignored her. 'I'll take the adjoining one. I'll just light the fires.'

Carrie could see he must have set them earlier, and within minutes they were both burning brightly, instantly reducing her sense of fear and bringing warmth to the rooms.

Massimo pulled something out of a set of drawers and handed it to her. 'They'll drown you, but they're all I have.'

It was a pair of pyjamas. His.

He said, 'There's some clean unused underwear in the drawers too. Again, far too big, but they'll do just until we get back to town.'

The thought of wearing Massimo's briefs, even if unused, sent an erotic thrill through Carrie. 'I'll be fine.'

'Here's another torch.'

Carrie misjudged the distance and the torch fell to the ground between them. She bent down to get it, and when she stood up again found Massimo was much closer. Suddenly it was hard to breathe.

The lines of his face looked much harsher in the flickering light of the fire. His eyes were totally dark and unreadable. He looked huge, too—a massive broad shape. With every cell in her body Carrie wanted nothing more than to step close and wind her arms around him, let him silence all the voices in her head with his mouth and his tongue and his body.

Carrie could almost feel him compelling her to do it. She just needed to take a step forward and he would catch her. It would be so easy…but it would make her forget why it was so important to resist his pull.

She took a step back. Massimo's jaw clenched.

She said, 'Goodnight, Massimo.'

'If you need anything during the night, I'm just through that door.'

'I won't…but thank you.'

Why did her voice sound so thready and unsure?

Disgusted with herself, Carrie watched Massimo disappear and shut the door behind him. She felt wide awake, keyed up. She found the en-suite bathroom and ran herself a bath. As promised by Sheila, the water was hot.

Carrie sank down into the water, relishing the feeling of weightlessness. She put a hand on her bump, but quickly diverted her thoughts when images of Massimo intruded. She was *not* going to humiliate herself again when he was mere feet away.

She quickly washed and stepped out, drying herself and pulling on Massimo's pyjamas. She didn't bother with the trousers as the top came halfway down her thighs.

She turned off the torch, climbed into the bed and fell into a fitful sleep that was dominated by dreams. Dreams of running through this house looking for something…or someone. In the dream she eventually she stopped outside a door and pushed it open. Massimo was in bed with his back to her. A woman's manicured hand was on his shoulder. He turned to look at Carrie and his expression was remote, cold.

'You are not welcome here. Get out.'

It was like a knife sliding through her ribs. White-hot pain and then red-hot jealousy. Carrie ran around the bed and pulled at the other woman, crying and saying, 'But I'm different…you told me I was!'

Carrie woke up and sat bolt upright, heart pounding.

Massimo's rejection of her was so vivid, the pain real.

She knew where she was, even though it was dark and the fire was low. She was breathing heavily. Her skin was hot and she was perspiring. She could still feel the strength of emotions running through her. The pain and the jealousy. The aching for Massimo to be in bed with *her*. No one else.

She didn't think.

She acted on an instinct too strong to deny.

She turned on the torch and got out of bed, went to the door. Hesitating for only the briefest of moments, she opened it and went into the next room.

Massimo was sprawled across the bed. Torso bare.

Sheets tangled around his waist. He looked as if he was in the throes of some dream too.

Carrie almost turned back, but at that moment Massimo woke up.

He came up on one elbow. 'Carrie?'

'Yes.'

'Are you okay?'

'I had a bad dream…but that's not it. I'm saying yes.'

'Yes, to what?' He sat up, threw the sheet back. He was naked.

'I want you.'

'Come here… I'm not sure if I'm dreaming or not.'

She walked over, dropping the torch as she did so. It sent its beam of light over the wall, illuminating faded wallpaper, but she didn't see that. She just saw Massimo, looking like a god, sitting on the bed.

She walked right up to him. There wasn't a moment of doubt in her head or body. This felt *right*. She couldn't even recall why she'd been so determined to deny herself now.

Massimo reached for her, taking her by the waist. Her much thicker waist. She wore nothing under the pyjama top. He started to undo the buttons and it fell open. Massimo sucked in a breath and Carrie's blood surged. She felt powerful under his burning gaze.

He cupped her fuller breasts, his thumbs moving over her nipples. She was so sensitive she trembled. Massimo pushed the pyjama top off completely and tugged her until she fell on the bed.

His hands roved over her whole body, learning the changes, rousing her to a fever-pitch of need. His mouth found her nipple, tugging it into his mouth, laving it with his tongue.

Carrie grabbed his head, her fingers tunnelling through his hair. Holding him. But then he moved down. His hand was on her belly now. Fingers spread wide. There was a reverence in his gaze that undid something inside her. Another defence that she knew she would have to rebuild tomorrow. But for now...

'Mass... *Please*... I need you.'

He moved down between her legs, spreading them so he could see her. Carrie's hips twitched. She had dreamt of this so much... And then he was there, his hot breath on her, fingers pushing her even wider as he bent his head and placed his mouth right on the core of her body, his wicked tongue pushing her over the edge of pleasure.

The waves were still ebbing when he moved over her, his erection in his hand, moisture beading the tip. For a moment he hesitated, and Carrie almost begged him again, but then he said, 'Is this okay...? Will I harm the babies?'

Carrie reached for him, greedy. 'It's fine...the doctor said it's fine.'

She might have been embarrassed if she hadn't been feeling so desperate.

Massimo was careful to keep his full weight off her even as he sank deep inside, and Carrie let out an almost feral sound. Slowly he moved, taking their bodies on a dance that was unique to them. Slow at first, and then fast and hard. Carrie wasn't ready for the next rush of pleasure. It caught her by surprise and she couldn't breathe for a long moment, aware of Massimo's body jerking against her and his own guttural sounds as he climaxed inside her.

Carrie woke as dawn was breaking outside, tucked into Massimo's embrace, her back to his front. She knew instinctively that he was awake too and without a word they made love again, without even changing position. He cupped her breast and put a hand between her legs, opening her up, and she gasped when he thrust deep and hard. When she came in a rush of pleasure Massimo tumbled just behind her, and as she fell asleep again she felt completely at peace and wondered faintly if she was still dreaming.

CHAPTER TEN

BUT IT HADN'T been a dream. When Carrie woke again the sun was high and Massimo was standing at the window. Dressed in his jeans again and a jumper. She felt thoroughly dishevelled, and deliciously sore between her legs.

He turned around and Carrie pulled the sheet up. It was a bit late for modesty, but she was hurtling into full-on regret and recrimination.

What had she done?

'Don't do that,' Massimo said.

'Do what?'

'Regret what happened.'

Carrie's face grew hot.

Massimo muttered, 'I knew it...'

Carrie sat up. 'Can you pass me a robe or something, please?'

Massimo plucked a robe off the end of the bed and handed it to her. He didn't look away as she got into it, and she hated it that her body responded to his unabashed gaze with such eagerness, her blood thrumming as if she hadn't just spent the night in his bed.

She got out of bed and tied the robe tightly around her. 'Do we have to have this conversation now?'

'It's as good a time as any.'

'Look, what happened last night... It's pregnancy hormones. It's common for women to feel more—'

'Horny?' Massimo supplied crudely.

'Something like that.'

'You're saying that's all it is?'

'Well, how would I know? I've been pregnant since the last time we slept together.'

Liar, whispered a voice.

She knew well it had nothing to do with being pregnant. And she knew she couldn't not be honest.

'No,' she admitted. 'Of course it's not just that. I've wanted you too.'

'There's something I need to tell you,' he said.

Instinctively Carrie sensed it was something she really didn't want to hear, but she said nothing.

He said, 'I've realised something over the past few months. I think I always knew, but I told myself that I just wanted marriage in order to provide security and stability...to offer our children a better life. But it's more than that. Carrie, I know what a bad marriage looks like. How much damage it can inflict on children. That's why I never wanted one. I felt sure I'd pass something on... the same destructive streak Ric and my parents had... But I know that's not rational. They reacted the way they did due to whatever dysfunction it was they experienced. But since meeting you...since being with you... I've seen how two people can communicate and be together. I want more, Carrie. I want it all. The chance to build a happy life together and for our children. But I won't settle for anything less than *all* of you.'

Carrie instinctively took a step back.

Massimo saw the movement and wouldn't let her escape his dark gaze.

'Carrie, I love you. Those six weeks without you after New York were torture. I missed you so much it was like a physical pain. And it wasn't just about the sex. You crept under my skin and into my heart. There's only one other person I have loved this much...'

Carrie was hearing his words but it was as if they were very far away. As if there was a glass shield between her and Massimo. She felt numb. Encased in ice.

Flashbacks were filling her head. Her husband saying, *'But I love you so much, Carrie. Marry me and I'll look after you always. You need me.'*

Past and present were tangled, and all Carrie could think was that she had to protect herself from being manipulated all over again.

Before Massimo could speak again, she said, 'You don't need to lie to get me to marry you, Massimo. If I decide to marry you it'll be for all the reasons you've already outlined.'

His jaw clenched at her rejection of what he'd said. 'So you're agreeing to marriage, then?'

'No,' Carrie said quickly, feeling claustrophobic. 'I mean, I haven't really thought it through...'

'Because you're scared. You're scared of losing yourself again—of handing over your agency to someone who will take advantage. But you're not that woman any more, Carrie. And I am not that man. You *know* this.'

It was as if he was reaching inside her and rooting through all her deepest insecurities, plucking them out to expose them to the bright daylight. She felt unbelievably threatened.

'Last night was a mistake,' she said.

'No, it wasn't. It was inevitable,' he said. And then, 'I'm not lying, Carrie. I'm not denying that people can use love to be manipulative and cruel, but what I feel for you isn't that. I told myself I'd never love again after losing Ricardo, and I was so careful. I never allowed any woman a chance to get close, and that worked fine—until you. The minute I touched you I knew it was different.'

Carrie wanted to put her hands over her ears. She wanted to block out Massimo's smooth words. The way they were winding around her like silken threads beckoning her to believe him. Trust him.

But her past loomed like a large, malevolent spectre behind her. Reminding her not to be so weak.

She looked at Massimo. 'I want to go back to London now.'

Tension crackled between them. When he spoke, Massimo's voice was as cold as she felt.

'Luckily, Tom has cleared the drive and most of the snow has already melted. We'll leave as soon as you're ready.'

Carrie fled the room on shaky legs. She closed the door between them and with a numb brain had a shower, avoiding looking at the faint marks of Massimo's hands on her body.

She dressed in her own clothes again and roughly dried her hair, pulling it back.

Downstairs, Massimo was waiting, grim. Sheila and Tom were there, and Carrie said goodbye to them. The older couple seemed to sense the tension and weren't overly chatty. Carrie was glad. Her emotions bubbled too close to the surface, raw and volatile.

The journey back into town was silent. But the tension was mounting to an unbearable pitch.

When they were driving through central London, not far from Massimo's house, Carrie acted on impulse. 'You can let me out here,' she told him.

'What? Here?'

There was an art gallery nearby—Carrie had recognised it. 'Please, Massimo, I just need some time on my own.'

With evident reluctance he pulled in at a safe spot and Carrie put her hand on the door.

He said, 'Wait, do you have your mobile with you?'

She nodded.

'Call me and I'll come and get you, okay?'

Carrie nodded and got out.

Massimo drove away. She could see him looking in the rear-view mirror and then he was gone.

She let out a shaky breath.

She headed for the art gallery, just wanting to lose herself in a crowd. Inside it was warm, and not that busy. There was an exhibition featuring Mexican artist Frida Kahlo, and on a whim Carrie bought a ticket.

She went in and within minutes, in spite of her own

turmoil, was transported into this fascinating woman's life.

Her early polio illness. The shattering bus accident when she was a teenager that left her with lifelong injuries and chronic pain. The passionate love affair with Diego Rivera that lasted until she died, in spite of many infidelities on either side.

She, too, had poignantly lost more than one pregnancy. And yet through it all she'd lived, loved and created. Her life force had been strong in spite of her many struggles. She hadn't cowered pitifully from the world, nor from the man who loved her—*really* loved her. She'd trusted. And she'd loved.

Love.

As if she had just needed to see it from another perspective, Carrie felt her heart crack open. She couldn't stop it. The walls of fear and defence she'd been clinging on to so desperately dissolved.

She'd never known love before—not like this. She'd had a toxic example of love. She'd known intellectually that she hadn't really loved her husband, or he her, but it had taken until this moment to really understand what real love looked like.

And that was why she'd been so scared. Because it was terrifying. And magnificent. And transformational. From the moment Massimo had first looked at her, four years ago, he'd unlocked something inside her.

She didn't even realise she was crying until a woman handed her a tissue and said, 'She's an inspiration, isn't she?'

Carrie could only nod.

Somehow, she stumbled out of the art gallery. She was undone. She was in pieces. But it felt okay. These were pieces she could use to put herself back together. She had no choice now but to trust, and she knew that no matter what happened she would be okay—because she was strong enough to withstand anything. Even Massimo telling her he loved her just to get her where he wanted her.

Because she loved him with every fibre of her being.

Massimo paced back and forth in the reception hall. He'd tried calling Carrie, but her phone was off.

He shouldn't have left her alone on the street.

He shouldn't have told her he loved her.

He'd spooked her.

It had been hours now. She could be anywhere.

The thought that he'd spooked her so much that she'd run away sent a chill down his spine. The thought of never seeing her again was terrifying.

It was getting dark outside.

Massimo was almost in full panic mode. He'd only been like this once before, when he'd seen his brother spin off that race track in Monte Carlo.

He was about to find his keys and get into his car to go and look for her when the gate intercom rang.

The butler appeared and Massimo snapped at him. 'I have it.'

He answered.

'Hi, it's me. I forgot my keys.'

Carrie.

Relief made Massimo feel shaky.

He pressed the buzzer and saw her slip through the gate. He could see her on the security monitor by the door. When she approached the front door he opened it—as she had done countless times for him.

The irony wasn't lost on him.

He tried to curb his panic when she came through the door. 'Where were you?'

She looked at him, and she had an expression on her face he couldn't decipher.

'Can we talk?' she asked.

Massimo nodded and closed the door and led her to his study. His relief was tempered now with the frustration he'd felt earlier, and anger at himself for saying what he had.

It was too soon.

She came in behind him and slipped off her coat, draping it over a chair. She looked wind-tousled. She looked beautiful.

The memory of her reaction earlier made him say, 'Look, Carrie, I don't want to pressure you into anything. I just—'

'Did you mean it?'

He looked at her. She was standing behind a chair and her hands were gripping the back of it. Knuckles white.

He went still inside. 'Did I mean what?'

'That you love me.'

Massimo knew that this moment counted for everything. If he couldn't convince Carrie of this, they didn't have a chance.

'Yes,' he said simply. 'I did. I would not use that word

to manipulate anyone. I have avoided using that word my whole life. I didn't even tell my brother I loved him, and I've always regretted that.'

Carrie's eyes looked suspiciously bright. 'I'm sure he knew.'

'Do *you* know? That's what's important here.'

'I'm no one special. I'm just your housekeeper.'

Massimo shook his head. 'You are the woman who has humbled me. No one else ever managed that because no one else ever interested me enough. I never wanted another woman beyond one night, and that made me arrogant...complacent. I thought I was in control. Then you came along and I realised I'd been fooling myself. I just hadn't met you.'

Carrie came out from behind the chair and took a small box out of her jeans pocket. She came over to stand in front of him. Her hands were trembling.

She opened the box to reveal a thick gold band. She looked up at him and said, in a voice full of emotion, 'Massimo Black... Linden... Earl, Lord, all that you are, will you please marry me?'

Massimo was in shock. Emotions were rushing through him, filling him and breaking him wide open. He shook his head faintly, 'None of that matters, and yes, I'll marry you but one condition.'

'What's that?'

'That you love me too. I want everything, Carrie. Your heart and soul and body and mind. And our babies.'

Carrie's eyes filled with tears. She smiled, and it was wobbly. 'You have me—heart, soul, body and mind. I love you, Massimo, and I've known it for so long. I was too afraid to admit it, because I knew that once I did I'd have no control over what happened... I was terrified to think that I'd repeat the mistakes of the past. I was afraid I'd be handing you power over me... It was all tangled up... I didn't want to be weak again.'

Massimo cupped her cheek with his hand. 'You were abused by a master manipulator, Carrie, and you paid the highest price. You were never weak and you are *not* weak. You're the strongest person I know.'

Massimo bent his head and kissed Carrie so softly and with such reverence that her heart cracked open all over again. The pain of the past dissolved completely, and the hope she'd been holding back expanded and filled every inch of her being.

When he pulled back she felt dizzy. She was still holding the box. She smiled at Massimo and took the ring out of the box, took his hand in hers. 'It's only a placeholder until you can choose your own ring,' she said.

'Shouldn't I be saying that to you?'

Carrie put the ring on his finger. It fitted perfectly. She wound her arms around his neck and pressed close. She lifted her face to his and said, 'We have time to say all the things...but first, make love to me, Mass.'

'Always, my love,' he breathed—and did exactly as she asked.

Massimo never did choose another ring. A month later they were married in a discreet civil ceremony in London, with Sheila and Tom from Linden Hall as their witnesses.

EPILOGUE

Two years and three months later, Rio de Janeiro

THE TWO SMALL bodies were sprawled side by side on the sunbed under the shade. They had just turned two the day before. They were sturdy and mischievous and demons and angels all at once. They both had dark hair, but Ricardo's eyes took after Carrie's, greenish hazel, and Frida's were dark, like her father's. And for a short time, blessedly, they were asleep.

Sheila and Tom had come with them to help look after the babies and to have a holiday. They'd become much beloved adoptive grandparents to the twins, and were now off on a tour for a couple of days.

Massimo and Carrie had kept Ricardo's penthouse apartment down on the beach for themselves, as a secret bolthole, but they'd bought a more practical villa-style house in a leafy suburb of Rio for the family.

Carrie sighed contentedly and settled back into Massimo's embrace on their own lounger. His arms were wrapped around her, their legs entwined.

She could feel the rumble of his chest against her

back when he said, 'You never did tell me why you wanted to call our daughter Frida.'

Carrie turned so that she was looking up at him. She traced the lines of his face with a finger. Love for this man filled her entire being. For everything he'd shown her about what love really was. Empowering and un-selfish and amazing.

She'd grown into herself in a way that still made her emotional, fully stepping into her power and her con-fidence. There were no dark corners any more, and if there were they worked through them together.

'I love you,' she said simply, the words flowing out easily.

Massimo took her hand and lifted it, kissing her palm. 'I love you too… Now tell me why you wanted to call our daughter Frida.'

Carrie smiled. It was one of the last secrets she'd kept from him… 'Well, do you remember the day I proposed?'

Massimo smiled too. 'The best day of my life? Of course.'

Carrie told him about the exhibition, and how it had opened her up and allowed her to be brave.

Massimo dropped her hand. 'You mean that if it wasn't for Frida Kahlo I'd still be chasing you and try-ing to get you to agree you love me too?'

Carrie chuckled. 'I was already caving by then… she just helped.'

Massimo put his fingers to his mouth and kissed them, sending the kiss to the sky. 'Thank you, Frida Kahlo.'

Carrie took Massimo's hand then, and brought it to her belly. She saw his eyes widen.

She nodded, feeling emotional. 'We'll have to start thinking of a new name soon.'

The pure joy on his face rippled through her too. But she was apprehensive. They'd been in such a little bubble since they'd married, and with the twins…

'What is it?' Massimo asked, of course seeing everything.

'Are we moving too fast?' she asked.

Massimo grinned and lay down, pulling Carrie over him. Her hair fell around them like a wild golden curtain.

Massimo twined some strands around his fingers.

'Not fast enough,' he said. 'Didn't I mention I want at least six children?'

Carrie groaned. 'Can I have the commitment-phobic man back, please?'

Massimo shook his head. 'That man is gone for ever. You ruined him.'

Carrie could feel his body responding under hers. After all, they were wearing minimal clothing. She in a bikini and him in swim-shorts.

She squirmed against him deliciously.

He groaned softly and kissed her, saying, 'You'll pay for that.'

Then Massimo sobered for a moment. 'I can't wait for our family to expand. The joy that you and Frida and Ric have brought me… I think what we're afraid of is that we can't take any more joy…'

Carrie felt emotional. 'Maybe that's it.'

He shook his head and smiled. 'There's no one else I'd want to be on this adventure with. You are the centre of my being, and as long as you're with me we can do anything.'

Carrie mock-growled at him. 'You'll never get rid of me.'

'Good.'

At that moment there was movement, and a small sleepy voice from nearby. 'Mama? Dada?'

Carrie and Massimo looked at one another, and then he said, 'Later, Lady Linden.'

She put on a look of mock outrage. 'I do believe that as you're an earl, I'm actually a countess.'

'I knew it—you only married me for my titles.'

Carrie laughed. 'Well, that and…'

She moved against him, and after one more indulgent kiss she got up to tend to the twins, who were both awake now.

Later, once the twins were asleep for the night, in the soft darkness under a tropical moon, they celebrated their news again, in a very private and intimate way.

Afterwards, deliciously sated and drowsy, Carrie pressed a kiss to the place between Massimo's neck and shoulder. 'I love you, Mass. For ever.'

He kissed her mouth and then put a hand on her belly. 'I love you. I love *us*. It's not too fast—it's perfect.'

And it *was* perfect.

* * * * *

Couldn't put
His Housekeeper's Twin Baby Confession *down?*
Then make sure to dive into these other
Abby Green stories!

The Flaw in His Red-Hot Revenge
Bound by Her Shocking Secret
Their One-Night Rio Reunion
The Kiss She Claimed from the Greek
A Ring for the Spaniard's Revenge

Available now!

#4129 INNOCENT'S WEDDING DAY WITH THE ITALIAN
by Michelle Smart

Discovering that her billionaire fiancé, Enzo, will receive her inheritance if they wed, Rebecca leaves him at the altar and gives him twenty-four hours to explain himself. He vows his feelings are real, but dare Rebecca believe him and succumb to a passionate wedding night?

#4130 THE HOUSEKEEPER'S ONE-NIGHT BABY
by Sharon Kendrick

Letting someone close goes against Niccolò Macario's every instinct. When he receives news that shy housekeeper Lizzie Bailey, the woman he spent one scorching night with, is pregnant, Niccolò is floored—because his only thought is to find her and claim his child!

#4131 BACK TO CLAIM HIS CROWN
Innocent Royal Runaways
by Natalie Anderson

When Crown Prince Lucian returns from the dead to reclaim his throne, he stops his usurper's wedding, creating a media frenzy! He's honor-bound to provide jilted Princess Zara with shelter, and the chemistry between the ruthless royal and the virgin princess sparks an urgent, irresistible desire...

#4132 THE DESERT KING'S KIDNAPPED VIRGIN
Innocent Stolen Brides
by Caitlin Crews

When Hope Cartwright is kidnapped from her convenient wedding, she's sure she should feel outraged. But whisked away by Cyrus Ashkan, the sheikh she's been promised to from birth, Hope feels something *far* more dangerous—desire.

HPCNMRA0723

#4133 A SON HIDDEN FROM THE SICILIAN
by Lorraine Hall

Wary of billionaire Lorenzo Parisi's notorious reputation, Brianna Andersen vowed to protect her baby by keeping him a secret. Now the Sicilian knows the truth, and he's determined to be a father! As their blazing chemistry reignites, Brianna must admit the real risk may be to her heart...

#4134 HER FORBIDDEN AWAKENING IN GREECE
The Secret Twin Sisters
by Kim Lawrence

Nanny Rose Hill is surprised when irresistible CEO Zac Adamos personally proposes a job for her in Greece looking after his godson! She can't let herself get too close, but can the innocent really walk away without exploring the unforeseen passion Zac has awakened inside her?

#4135 THEIR DIAMOND RING RUSE
by Bella Mason

Self-made billionaire Julian Ford needs to secure funding from a group of traditional investors. His solution: an engagement to an heiress, and Lily Barnes-Shah fits the bill perfectly! Until their mutual chemistry makes Julian crave something outside the bounds of their temporary agreement...

#4136 HER CONVENIENT VOW TO THE BILLIONAIRE
by Jane Holland

When Sabrina Templeton returns to the orphanage from her childhood to stop her former sweetheart from tearing it down, playboy CEO Rafael Romano offers a shocking compromise... He'll hand it over if Sabrina becomes his convenient bride!

YOU CAN FIND MORE INFORMATION ON UPCOMING HARLEQUIN TITLES, FREE EXCERPTS AND MORE AT HARLEQUIN.COM.

HPCNMRB0723

HARLEQUIN
PLUS

Try the best multimedia subscription service for romance readers like you!

Read, Watch and Play.

Experience the easiest way to get the romance content you crave.

Start your **FREE TRIAL** at
<u>www.harlequinplus.com/freetrial</u>.